The Honor System

WHERE CATHERINE AND I FIRST BUMPED INTO EACH other — where she backed into me — was on a shadowless expanse of desert floor in Death Valley National Monument, probably sixty miles' clearance in any direction. Friends consider this a new standard of clumsiness. They ask if it was tourist season, try to form pictures of foot traffic. It wasn't tourist season. This was at Badwater (Lowest Point in the Western Hemisphere), a crusty green pool that shrinks optically by fantastic degrees the closer you approach from the hills. It disappointed waves of nineteenth-century prospectors making the tearful, weaving descent to what had promised to be a stupendous reservoir of blue.

Today a highway stretches by the site to the turnout where Catherine's sport wagon from Don Garp Studio City sat cooling its engine noisily, a crystal pot under the hood. In front of the car, a wooden information post in the style of a birdhouse offered Department of the Interior historical pamphlets for 50 cents on the honor system. That proposition had Catherine literally swaying. She had only a five-dollar bill; she wanted a pamphlet very much. You wondered if similar ethical questions had given her trouble in Studio City. You wondered things like that in Death Valley, because there was time to imagine the stories behind people. The truth was, Catherine had left Studio City in a divorcée trance—grabbing on to the first inspiration that came, which was that manners were going to exempt her from the ambiguities of life and distance would keep her out of "situations" somehow. She'd ironed all her dresses in a single evening and for two days had been touring Death Valley in a variety of them, smoothing creases. Finally, she made it to Badwater and got herself hypnotized by this 50¢ Donation sign, which is where I found her when I arrived, second in line. It sounds ridiculous, but that is how we were: Catherine behind dark glasses, breathing these high, swaying breaths, and me waiting my turn, dismally. Until at some point she wasn't swaying so much as backpedaling; I had to say "Whoa," as a warning, and our feet got tangled up.

Saying "Whoa" instead of "I'm sorry" is something my Westwood therapist would call growth. I'm more skeptical about it. I felt sorry the way men habitually feel sorry, part of a consciousness of being clumsy around facts of suffering; learning a new noise to make before falling down doesn't seem like big growth to me. How funny the fall must have looked—two people basically sitting down with a backward running start, Catherine throwing her handbag up in the air like a pizza—occurred to me belatedly. Nowadays I can laugh picturing it. I can divide it into its phases. It seems to me every fall has one truly great moment, a kind of awakening: you hit dirt and lie there a second, and the planetary silliness of everything comes up through the ground. That was when Catherine pushed her sunglasses back and blinked up at me like a screen star, for laughs, playing a scene about someone falling into someone's arms; I flashed back to a childhood game, the one where you fall down on purpose (could you play London Bridge in the desert?), and I wanted to fall again. But I didn't say so, and in the next interval I couldn't have known *how* to; we remembered we were strangers. You could see this realization come over Catherine, too. She stopped fluttering her eyes, because the screen-star bit hadn't gotten a laugh. She then hid her face in her hands and pretended to gag. She was on her elbows, next to me. This all happened in a second or two.

"No," I said. "It was very funny."

"What?" She looked at me. "Oh."

I wasn't sure we'd even understood each other. I looked away, feeling foolish.

"Oh, God," she said suddenly. Her eye picked out a loose thread on her dress and she broke it off, started smoothing some creases, and gave up. Then she slid herself back to a position against the base of the information post, with her head propped back, mock-seductively. She was acting again, playing someone whose bell had really been rung. She took an elaborate, heartsick breath and smiled. "Well—good-bye."

What was I supposed to say? It was one routine after another. My father views that sort of person as a "type"—the "type who's afraid you'll leave before they think of what they wanted to say" is how he puts it. At which I roll my eyes, if only by habit; I want that sort of insight to come from someone I have more in common with, like my sister, the screenwriter. But conversations with my sister only turn out wishful: we fantasize people into the mysteries we want them to be, fearless and unknowable, parentless. It frightens me to admit that my father's is the more loving view of human nature; I have no idea how he came to it. I took a pamphlet and walked past Catherine, to the edge of the pond, pretending to study the insect life under the surface. ("The wigglers are the larvae of the Soldier Fly.") Sunset was crossing the valley a hue at a time, and I stood there until I heard Catherine drive away.

My father is also my boss. He is the only surviving swimming-pool contractor on Ventura Boulevard in Sherman Oaks, which used to be the capital of the business, wall-to-wall showrooms. Now he stands at the window and points at the boulevard with his mug of chicken soup. "That's where National Pool was," he will say, "before it folded in '66." They *all* folded in '66; it was the year my father scored his knockout punch. He'd been a landscape architect for Artists' Pool and Patio (today Artists' Patio) and noticed something everyone else missed, which was that all the pools in the San Fernando Valley were virtually touching each other. (He was on an airplane at the time.) The only markets left to expand into were hillsides and custom improvements, which coincidentally were my father's twin loves at the drawing board; stainless-steel pools, pools shaped like highball glasses, pools on stilts, canyon feats. Within ten months, the entire industry fell to him like spilled poker chips. He hired all the out-of-work architects, and there's been little for him to do since. I am being groomed to inherit the business. I stand at the window next to him for as long as I can take it and then tell him I think I'll take a few days off and go to Death Valley, probably my third time in a month. He doesn't seem to care. He reminds me to "look up Ed Gurstone" for him. It's the same conversation every time; my father has never even *met* Ed Gurstone, but according to a computer printout of his, they are both Lainie Kazan Fan Club chapter presidents, with Ed holding down Death Valley. Not even an address given, just the chapter name: the 4,000-Foot Club. I tell my father I think it's pointless, but he won't listen; he is convinced Ed Gurstone is out there. By now, he has me conditioned. I will be driving up an absolutely barren incline, pass a sign that says ELEVATION 3,900 FEET, and a voice in my head will say, "Slow down."

I've domesticated Death Valley with my routines—a place to sleep, a place to drink my coffee, a place to read, traveling from one simpleminded station to the next, a toy train set on a billiard table. Of course, nothing is sacred about this program except to me. It's possible to share the same valley and carry an entirely different map. One afternoon I was packing my car and saw from the road a German man with zinc oxide on his nose positioning his wife for a snapshot on the sand dunes—the Place Where I Sleep. But how were they to know that? Every night I throw down my bedding there, wake up at seven exactly, see the faces of the dunes stitched with the tracks of sidewinders. Every morning for one dollar I shower by the Amigos Campground swimming pool, tiptoe over fishy puddles chowdered with toilet paper, comb my hair in the scored mirror over the sink. The place where I pray faces a jet-black hill covered with milky tumbleweeds—white-on-black, stunned, like an X-ray photograph. My second sighting of Catherine was at this spot. I found it one day after Badwater. It had seemed at once a mountain and its own afterimage; I saw it with my mind's eye and I could hit it with a stone. The effect was supernatural. I looked back at my footprints and the tire marks beyond them, and saw for the first time that the desert held a record of me, and always would, that there was no escaping my tracks, that I was either graceful or I wasn't; and in that instant of neutrality, I guessed that I was. For an abstract idea it came to me pretty literally. I spent the next half hour clomping around in circles, admiring my own steps. I stretched my fingers out at the sky. I lined up objects in my view, pretending I could blast them with a look; my eyes ran a line a mile long, over the highway and the salt flats and a dry riverbed, and then straight into the last thing I expected to see, specifically, Catherine's sunglasses.

The instant of recognition startled the hell out of us both. In fact, I thought I could see her shudder, if you can see a shudder from the better part of a mile — it may have been a shadow, passing fast from a plane. Or it may have been nothing, just imagination, and my next thought was that Catherine couldn't see me at all, that her eyes were fixed miles past me on a mirage, or straight down at a snake — possibilities that were erased with a single stroke when Catherine crossed her heels and, smoothly, curtsied. At me. She held the curtsy a long time, while I waved my Dodgers cap in salute, and when it ended, I went off, tossing the cap up and down all the way to my car.

That seemed to begin a flirtation. A strange one, considering the distances involved. Sometimes we would signal with a flash of headlights. Sometimes I would watch Catherine's sport wagon reflecting the sun, sliding down a mountain road like a flame on a slow fuse. We did everything but come close enough to talk. We played gunfighters at five hundred yards, hands on holsters. We played photographers, Catherine advancing in a crouch, holding her sunglasses across her eyes like an Instamatic (a routine that was murder on her creases). A couple of days of this and I began to sleep badly. I would wonder what was going to come next in the game — blocking out scenes, resenting myself for devoting so much apparently romantic thought where there was so little basis. I would curse and try to sleep on my other side.

Then I would find myself replaying our first meeting. That Catherine and I met the way we did appealed to me for superstitious reasons. One, it was what the movie industry calls a "cute meet," which meant to me that we were destined to be together. We owed it to the movies. Two, lovers who met that way were nicely unprepared—having no chance to arrange themselves in the mirror of their fears. Here the realization that I had just thought my father's thought turned me over on my other side again. Whether real love was involved at all in my thoughts about Catherine I couldn't say. Once, when I was driving back from Scotty's Castle, a museum in the northern hills, I heard a radio therapist say there was no such thing as "growing to love." Only I didn't get to hear the concept he came up with to replace it. He was using a myth-versus-fact style of presentation and he was shouting, "There—is—no—such—thing—as—'growing—to—love' (interminable pause). . . . I'll say it again." The program was called *The Mental Health Hour*. Talk Radio is big for some reason in Death Valley, despite some primitive production values and despite the fact that there is virtually no audience to phone in. Which leaves the therapist pretty much to his own rhythms, save for a sound engineer who likes to fill the silences with a tape recording of pounding surf. Little thought has been given to how idiotic pounding surf sounds in Death

Valley; we get wave after wave. My problem this day was the mountain terrain: every time I rounded a curve, I lost the signal in the rocks. ". . . Lesson is this: Whomsoever you love," the man said—it was a favorite word of his, "whomsoever"—and then I would round a canyon wall and hit dead air. "Whomsoever, whomsoever, whomsoever!" And then, snowbanks of silence. Whomsoever I love, what? I was counting on reaching some open stretch of land at the critical moment of his thesis. As it happened, my car flew at the critical moment into a deep neck of road that may once have been a Borax mine. No daylight in sight. I made a desperate three-point turn and tried to get back to where I'd been, sliced the radio needle back and forth across the band, but never recovered the voice. At a turnout at the top of the hill, ten thousand feet up, where it is cold, I parked my car and stood in a stiff wind to stare across the valley; instantly this hit me as a trite pose, my hands in the pockets of my parka, and my heartsick sigh, like Catherine's heartsick sigh at Badwater, the difference being that hers was intended for a laugh. Over all of these things I lost sleep. Our every posture seemed big and important. The valley enlarged small lives.

Finally, I saw Catherine up close again. By accident. With just enough time gone by for me to have worked up a personal sense of ultimatum, of what-gives? Catherine was towel-drying her hair at the washbasin by the pool at Amigos Campground, around noon on a Sunday, and when she saw me she got cute right away. She shook her wet hair down over her eyes. "Small world," she said. "Question mark."

I nodded. Some teenagers who work at the ranch were drinking beers in the shallow end of the pool. German men bobbed in the deep end (German tourists love the American West), their gawky, topless wives reading novels in chaises by the Coke machine. Catherine was not topless. She wore a green bikini under a man's dress shirt, and without even stopping to think, I asked her, "Whose shirt?"

She blushed.

"Never mind," I said. "I'm sorry."

"This shirt?" she said. "This shirt belongs to a wealthy man who says I remind him of the girl who baby-sat him when he was a boy in Morocco." She snapped shut a compact mirror and looked me in the eye. "It's my husband's shirt. Ex-husband's. And I'd forgotten the association. You could have asked me anything else and the subject would never have come up." She looked down and when she raised her eyes again, she shook a finger at me. "So, nice going."

And then we were quiet, while I watched her at the mirror. She buttoned up the shirt, slipped out of her bathing-suit top from inside, and stashed it in a beach bag, both of us trying to act very modern and indifferent, and failing; finally, she let out all her air at once and had to lean on the basin with her forearms.

"Why are you so bold with me when you're far away?" I said.

"Why are *you?*"

"Well, I'm willing to get to know you right here."

She coughed. "Oh. Until *I* am, you mean. I mean, how convenient a thing for you to say when I'm already walking away. You know?"

"Huh?" I said.

"Let's understand each other. You're beginning to have a crush on me."

I shifted my weight onto the other foot and a few seconds went by and I shifted my weight back onto the original foot. "No, I'm not," I said.

She made a hopeless expression. "You *act* like you are," she explained. "You smile constantly. Without even blinking. You wave that . . . *cap.*"

"You started it!" I said. "It's a Dodgers hat."

"And boy, oh boy, you ran with it."

"So?"

"So!" She buried her face in her hands. She looked up suddenly, pained. "It really smells in here." And she whirled off to the pool, past it; I swept back one side of my hair in the mirror and took off behind her. She kept twenty yards between us. I walked faster. She walked faster. She entered the camp cafeteria, passed rows of green Jell-O in a trot; I trotted past green Jell-O. She zigzagged through the aisles and the tables, and had me good and beat when she reached the far door, put a hand on it, and looked up at the sign above, EMERGENCY EXIT ONLY. She froze. I caught up, and she hung her head.

So we went for a walk, beyond the camper stalls, toward the road. A hot wind had come up, bullying the sides of tents. Here Catherine told me about her Studio City life and told me her name and told me that her approach with a man had always been to play coy and lead him along, later to call his bluff by pointing out that he was mainly addicted to the chase, the same as she was. The routine afforded each of Catherine's men a graceful and dramatic exit. By the time she met Ramsey, she thought it was foolproof, and was getting extravagant with her good-byes. "I'm saying good-bye to someone I could spend my life with," Ramsey had said to her. And she replied, "If only you'd told me." They shook hands, and then he hung on to her hand for a moment and said, "Well, *I'm telling you*." They stood there and then embraced, miserably, each realizing the gravity of the mistake. She had no idea how she was going to hold his interest now. In a wedding picture taken just after the pronouncement and the kiss, both their mouths hung wide. From there, they went on what seemed like an ironic vacation: a honeymoon to try and patch things up. On the first night, Catherine danced ten dances with a college freshman and Ramsey slept with an actress. Finally, they had a dramatic good-bye that stuck. (Ramsey said, "I love you too much to put you through this.")

That was six months ago, Catherine said. She assured me that if I had a crush on her, it was only a crush on her "act," because what else did I have to go on? Her own question incited her. What the hell else do you have to go on? She said, and then clutched her stomach. She was nauseous. It had started at the washbasin and gradually gotten worse; when she finished sentences now, she was adding the comment "—dizzy." At which we both had to pause, there in the driveway, wind rattling the campground gate. "I'll be all right when we get to the highway," she said. "These faces dancing around. It's like in a telephoto lens."

At the highway, she was not all right. At the highway, it was chaos—the illness and the wind outdoing each other, a hysterical duet. Catherine walked backward, with her arms folded under her ribs; I trudged toward her through sheets of sand; a thick beige dust from the valley floor was swelling at the horizon like bread dough. We were having a civilized argument: I kept yelling, asking why Catherine wouldn't stand still for two seconds so I could catch up, and Catherine kept yelling, asking what I thought love was. Specifically, Catherine's argument was that you could not love a person when you hadn't seen the "real" person, and my argument was, didn't she think it worked the other way around: that love came first, and then if you were open to the idea, love automatically saw through to the "real" person, the person it intended to love. She stared at me, fighting to keep her shirt flat. "Whomsoever," I said. I was gesturing at clouds.

"You're really full of it," she finally said.

Some sand lashed my cheeks. "Wait up!" I called.

She pointed across the road. "We can talk in my car!"

"What about your stomach?"

She searched around with her fingers for pain, looked at me. She shrugged.

Ed Gurstone is a stout, pink-faced man with smooth white hair firmed back in rows, like a half dozen ladyfingers. Not that I had any idea in advance what the man was supposed to look like. It was his Winnebago that identified him for me. Catherine and I had ducked into her station wagon to talk, and then more or less noticed we didn't need to; our willingness to resolve things was as good as having done it. We just held hands in the front seat with our eyes closed, reliving what had happened already. Listening to sand sprinkle the windshield. Suddenly I had an intuition and opened my eyes. In the rearview I saw it: a wide-load motor home straining around a bend, in that harried, anthropomorphic way that motor homes strain around bends; then it barreled down the straightaway, close enough for me to make out the bullhorns on the roof and the hot-red lettering across the front; L-A-I-N-I-E. I practically threw myself under the wheels flagging him down.

A lot of shouted apologies and running about, and finally Gurstone helped us inside. He didn't share my sense of emergency about the errand, but he was polite. He made coffee and wrote down a post office box number to give to my father. From then on, the three of us just sipped coffee, staring out of opposite windows, trying to think of something to talk about. "I imagine it simplifies things, being the only member of the 4,000-Foot Club," I said, all of us nodding; Gurstone thought for several seconds and finally turned out his palms. "Well, the buck stops here!" he said. He exploded with laughter. A second later, we were all sipping our coffees and gazing in opposite directions again. "I used to live in town," Gurstone said. "But living here keeps things basic. I'm a remedial sort of person."

So am I, and Death Valley is always teaching me one lesson or another—though recently picturing the desert has had to take the place of going there. That is a good sign. It shows, for one thing, that my job has become tolerable to me; I've even started to put some imagination into it. Promotions and things. The county museum tribute to pool culture this year—that was my idea. Also, I've been handing my father a series of preposterous landscaping challenges, which have put him back at the drawing board, with his Walkman on, late into the night. I see Catherine most nights. We're "dating," but taking slow steps, for her sake. She is more cautious about involvements than I am. Here is where my memories of Death Valley serve me well. I picture us at Badwater, where things are so irreducible: Catherine and me and the land, and my superstitions of destiny—Gurstone is the wild card in this arrangement, his Winnebago careening sometimes into view, across the background, at the instant of our fall. It is as if my involvement with Catherine began at the ending, the essence—a notion that lifts me again and again to feelings of good faith. We almost never fight. Catherine might make us late for a movie, say, by taking too long to iron a dress — and instead of getting irritated about it, I'll simply think, Badwater. Then things blow over. It's a practical aid to life.

The Idols of Sickness

HARDLY ANYONE OPENS A MEDICAL ENCYCLOPEDIA who isn't looking for trouble. I can still see the malformed children with their eyes censored and some of them actually seemed to be smiling, maybe at their parents off-camera, as if they had been promised a surprise. The photos were black and white and shadowy, and the boys looked taxidermic with their early twentieth-century haircuts, standing naked and listing to the side with the full-grown arm. There were time sequences of genital buds trying to emerge into penises from shrouds of hair grown by injections. The book was old enough that many of the boys had undoubtedly died before I saw them when I was eleven.

Yet I felt I knew them, or they knew me. I have always felt drawn to a land of bad dreams. The walnut desk in our den where the book sat faced a window onto the backyard, where eucalyptus leaves floated in the pool and no one was swimming. My older sister may have been tanning in one of the rusty lounges on the side of the patio that I couldn't see.

My new bad habit in those days was to breathe wrong. When no one was around, or when no one suspected, squeezing out air seemed to bring a sense of reassurance, like the act of twitching a sore muscle. You'd enclose the airlessness like a moth under a cup until your abdomen almost met your lower back. For a fleeting window of time in the 1960s, I took the reflex to freak-show levels — all but swallowing myself up under my rib cage with a lower set of muscles. Our mother, a Clairol hair-color model, was in New York with a truck driver boyfriend on a shoot. With or without her, the house was as neglected as an attic. I walked from room to room violating the privacy of her letters and scrapbooks and making my stomach disappear before the mirror. Having a trick that only I could really excel at seemed to epitomize the liquid luck of being young. At the same time, I was concerned — I knew that the miracle of the body wasn't supposed to be monkeyed with, and there were frequent occasions when I tightened up too much and the testicles crawled up inside my stomach, so I began keeping the whole thing a secret, although secrecy made the habit continue.

I did tell Steve Breitenbach once. I told Breitenbach everything. He thought I was funny, loco, cheered me on, even the times when he knew I was lying. I had exaggerated plenty of times to entertain him — about animals I'd seen die, or things I'd overheard between my mother and the truck driver. I had told him that our hi-fi had erupted into flames under a stack of ten Stones records.

But privately I felt troubled about the children in the photos. Captured for all time in that haunted state. Throw out the photographic record, and sickness might be only a perturbance, the shadow of a cloud if not a misperception completely, and here some doctor's photographer had caught it, ghost-like, documenting evil for generations of physicians. The pages were dusty and heartless. No one in the house had been known to open the book but me.

There was one patient, dark and dumb like a miniature gangster or a Marx brother, one of those kids who steals to survive and weasels out of things, and when he cries to his mom, cries a big roaring cry. I would never have liked him in school. Just like you wouldn't have chosen your cousins. What you got from reading the text about him bordered on horticulture. I remember Latin words ending in *-is* and *-ids*, like names for bulbs or canals. Ultimately, injections of hormones carried him through puberty. The testicles descended, and none too soon, because his inguinal opening had gradually sealed, closing the old passage to the abdominal cavity. I was flexing myself down and up spontaneously and squeezing out breath at the very moment that I read about his narrow escape.

The next sentence was the bad one for me. It named a related nonclosure through which an unlucky boy could trap his own testicles. It was one of those sentences you read over and over wondering how you made the wrong turn that got you to where you were, sitting in a room, unraveling your fate. There was no way back and the future hung in limbo. It was about eleven in the morning and my sister came inside from the patio, and I slid the book into the desk drawer memorizing a page number that was up above a thousand and walked into my mother's vacant bedroom, ten feet away but it felt like two hundred yards, dropping myself solemnly on top of her bedspread to think and to be scared. You could see the pool from her window, too, and hear the kids in a neighbor's pool laughing, yelling, and diving.

When it was dark I composed a note for my mother. "Oh mom," it began. I was as thorough as a prosecutor, bulleting sentences and citing the pages in the medical encyclopedia that dealt with the condition of pseudocryptorchonids.

In addition to being a haircolor model, our mother could be the most wonderful listener in the world, half the time — magical, tender, and filled with compassion. Confiding in a beautiful mother was best when you were convinced that this time you had fallen beyond her aid, and you told her everything, to prove that it was so. But it's not exactly true that the sick choose sickness, for they want someone to save them from themselves.

During the three days before she would get back from New York, I kept getting up in the night to insert additional evidence into the note or escalate the language, closing every loophole for hope. I checked constantly on my abdominal trick too, hoping vaguely to find out that the quirk had gone away, or maybe persuade myself that it wasn't anything dangerous, because what came up also came down. But instead I detected a new scary friction.

My sister got tired of making breakfast and started giving me money I could spend at the Little League concession stand. So Breitenbach and I took off one morning on our bikes, and I whispered, "Get this. That trick I told you I could do isn't a talent, it's a defect!"

Breitenbach was as ready as a mirror to buy in to this—when I laughed with holy panic, so did he. Possibly he was embarrassed. He was the smooth one of the neighborhood, and he didn't need me as a friend except for the fact that he needed everyone in the neighborhood as a friend. He was good company, singing, "Jameson, man, this could only happen to you."

We stayed a long time at the Little League carnival, talking to some girls. I postponed being alone as long as I could because I knew what was good for me, but I seriously wanted to hide at home. The day seemed strung with ballasts and weights. It was bright but not clear, like summer in the south before a storm—evacuation weather.

We got in the Hammerhead and asked the carny to spin our car upside down before the ride started. "Do you got a pussy?" the carny said. "The boss says I can't give an extra spin unless you got a pussy." The ride jerked forward, contorting through the sky. It could heave you around for all it was worth and three minutes wouldn't have passed. Carnivals are the world's worst escapes.

What hope I had rested on the knowledge that

my mom would be back late that night. The note lay alive on her pillow, and I expected to be in bed pretending sleep when she read it, but I dozed before she got there, and then she was sitting on the edge of my bed leaning over to kiss me.

"You could have called the hotel," she said.

Already I felt ashamed that this urgency was in her. The lamplight from the den vectored through another path of light in the hall and I heard the couch cushions sigh. It occurred to me that the truck driver was also in the house.

Clearly my mother was puzzled, and she began to confer with me the way she would with another adult. "Listen, duck, I showed your note to Jim, I hope you don't mind — just because I don't understand anything about being a boy." The boyfriend was out there knowing my entire situation. "And he'd never heard of it either, but he asked a good question. He wondered, doesn't *pseudo* imply that it's not the real disease?"

"No. It's very clear from the text. Did you read the book?"

"As much as we could understand."

"Pseudo might mean the state of being hidden, instead of being missing at birth. It's still an abnormality."

"Try not to worry." She didn't smile, nor was she trying to be cold. "We can go to Kaiser, but you'll just have to try to leave it alone. Tough it out." She made a fist. "You can do it."

No boy wants to be told by his mother that the time has come to tough it out — as if she despairs that he knows how, or that she can get the point across in the foreign tongue of a father or coach. She was trying to imitate her own father, long dead and so legendary to her that his toughness was all the more untranslatable.

Nor did she have faith in any God to speak of, except the God who helps those of us who help ourselves. The glow from the hall silhouetted our failure, and a collapse of effort settled in that first felt almost like boredom. As long as a mother lives, she will believe in your crises — a conspiracy that is beautiful but changes nothing in the vastness of the night. I could hear her dress shift on the bed and an earring jangle. And a cough from the boyfriend in the den. I was as good as alone here. I had taken things too far. I began to coach myself as she sat on the bed. She would leave any moment and take comfort with her, but that was the beauty of comfort. Even a life of wanting could seem perfectly endurable broken down to its moments. I put this faith together in case nobody was ever going to help me. I had all these nights ahead to be responsible for my own peace of mind, and never to perform my genital trick again.

Then puberty sealed the passages in my body until I couldn't revert if I tried, and I had the long legs and ankles of a surfer Jesus. I had girls in my bed all of a sudden, two of them kicking over my surfboard one night, scaring my mom though not bringing her to my room. In the mornings I swam through the eucalyptus leaves in the pool like a Roman in the aqueducts.

In high school, Breitenbach broke his neck jumping off a high-dive but recovered, giving buddies a story to tell. Daredevils like Evel Knievel were interviewed on television in their body casts, proving that a body is only a body. These were people who seemed to have no spiritual leanings at all. Whereas I found a guitar and tried religion, and a youth pastor told me that the body was just a tool for communication, so it didn't strictly belong to me. This made sense only if you were as frightened as I was, starved for sense, and maybe not even then. My hope was to slip in and out of the pastor's belief, depending on how many pleasures I could still collect by owning my body for myself.

But my mood can turn like the weather, and when leaves and acorns drift on the surface of my pool I inevitably seem to hear a bass note in the sound track of summer that none of our guests ever hears. I married a girl from San Diego and we drink wine on our patio above the nude beach at La Jolla, a town halfway between naval history and Pablo Neruda. My mother died in her sixties, leaving a profitable modeling agency to my sister and me. All the furnishings from my childhood are right there inside the house—the walnut desk, the couch, and the lamp that stays on past the hall. The medical encyclopedia with all the children and dwarfs is too beautiful and weird to get rid of, but too ancient and torn to display. It's on the bottom shelf of the bookcase in the hall, by the room where my ten-year-old sleeps.

Sonority

YOU NEVER SEE ANN REALLY LET HERSELF DANCE; IN lieu of it, she gives little imitations. These last a couple of seconds at a time. She rattles her head like pills to the power chords, agreeing with nothing. Choking on volts. But she comes out of it each time sighing, a pleased smile under her long, clever nose. "That kind of dance," she says. "That pantomime, locking out time. That's what you do." *Me?* I pretend to search myself. I don't want to know "what you do." I want Ann just to do it. Instead, she has another two-second attack. She holds an imaginary mike to the chins of some bewildered, thrashing kids and pulls away laughing. Then she runs across the dance floor to me, her dark bangs flying, and steals the notepad from my coat. *Fighting the music,* she writes, *because you don't want it to end*—flashes it once in my face like a credential; I'm still seeing the words after the pad is tucked away. *Fighting the music.* I touch Ann's hair, savoring the nice description.

Apparently Ann likes the line too, because twenty minutes later I overhear her using it on Chuck.

(Chuck is this band manager Ann wants to impress; he recently hired her to design some album covers.) Not that I have to eavesdrop. Ann doesn't mind if I know everything about her, all her plans and designs. Or she tells herself that in some sense I already do, a concept she considers a relief. Letting one friend in on her sins is Ann's compromise with guilt. The thought of one person "understanding." I fell into the role by what seems like a ludicrous coincidence. Someone had given me a religious pamphlet called *Understanding,* and I was trying it out. That isn't the gist of a story — it is the whole story. I remember the pamphlet almost photo-graphically. "Understanding Evil," "Understanding Famine," "Understanding Perplexity," and what seemed to be a high number of cartoon illustrations, leaping with question marks: Understanding was the answer to it all. This was last fall, in Los Angeles — "The autumn of your Christ-like stare," my brother calls it. I would read my pamphlet and my newspaper over hot-and-sour soup at Chao Praya, world events rolling off my shoulders. One day, Ann walked in irritably and asked if I thought I could share. I offered her the View section and she said, *The table.*

People are always surprised to find out I'm younger than Ann — by three months, but younger just the same — because I act so comparatively reserved. I'm not sure what to make of that analysis; I used to strike people as "defeated," so possibly it's a step up. It seems to me that from the start Ann and I were equally tired, but of different things.

She was tired of defending herself, and I was tired of my expectations. I was tired of voting even, if that relates, it was the first year I didn't register, although I made the mistake of keeping a tally, and all my causes and candidates lost, except for one initiative, which according to an exit poll a majority of voters misunderstood on account of a double negative. There is a point where hopelessness and strength look like the same thing on me. Four, five days into our Chao Praya phase, Ann was working herself up, reading me her stone-faced riot act, warning me she was a disaster, and sad, and a cheat, and no friend of mine, and on about some vitamins she'd been stealing from her roommate just to see if he'd forgive her; she had eaten three multitabs already today.

What I did was throw my wallet on the table. My wallet and then my car keys, and the pamphlet, too. I just pushed it all across the table and touched Ann's hair (our first time). I kept hearing the voice of a television car salesman: I will eat my tie, I will stand on my head and stack dimes at the corner of Sunset and Vine. It was supposed to be a powerful stunt, my renunciation of things material. I wanted to say, "It's all right." But then the words seemed overly literal, and I was stuck there with my hand through the leaves of a centerpiece, smoothing Ann's bangs and wondering all at once how it was, how it actually was that people talked to each other. It's hard to describe the gravity of what I was feeling—that sense of injustice all tied up with love. It was less a matter of loving Ann than an almost anonymous love wish for her, wanting Ann to feel loved without me in the way. And all the trite futility of that.

Which, at any rate, has made us a kind of tragic marvel in the eyes of our friends, a modern Jake and Brett. For the record, I don't like being told that what I've been doing all these months with Ann is protecting myself, that when I say I don't want to demand things of Ann, I supposedly mean I don't want to care. Generally the unspoken topic here is sex. At about three months, I think it was, sex became an option for us. Just an option, and then it seemed to stop. What had made it possible in the first place was the innocence: Ann was crying about something that frightened her, a medical scare one of her sisters had had—Ann didn't even know how scared she'd been until it turned out to be a false alarm—and I was holding her, by her kitchen sink, feeling so young and ordinary and loyal; it was a hot day and Ann's cheek was tear-streaked, her face broken out, and just for a moment it seemed (paradoxically) erotic to think that there was nothing separating us, that nothing held a sexual charge.

Then the phone rang in the hall and it was Ann's friend Helen, this publicist who throws terrible theme parties. Helen is the biggest matchmaker of the bunch. ("Is that who I think it is, coughing in the background?") I guess the popular demand finally killed it for us. Ann made a joke, about how she could do absolutely anything she put her mind to, until she thought it was required of her.

Back then, Ann couldn't bring herself to show this guy Chuck her artwork. She was reluctant even to approach him in Helen's backyard and hand him a business card (on Pearl Harbor day—a luau). The alibi was always college: Ann felt she had been cheated of something essential, some notion of a training ground for adulthood, because after both her older sisters went through Berkeley, the money ran out; her father got sick. Ann was only eight and got her image of higher education from the pictures in her sisters' yearbooks: For years she thought you had to wear the mortarboards to class. My question was, What *wasn't* a training ground, when you thought about it? I confronted Ann, there in the moonlight, at Helen's. What made her think life was anything but? "It's all Berkeley," I said. "Think of it as Berkeley." I can get a little electrified some-times—a transformation that makes Ann practically applaud, bouncing on a sofa and disregarding on the spot the substance of whatever it is I'm talking about. Ann glided over to Chuck in her grass skirt and presented her card, as kindly and effortlessly as if it were a scrap he had dropped and she was returning. I watched from across the lawn, feeling a certain pulse of empathy, trying to decide if she was using the Berkeley trick. Wondering if that was what leveled her out. And later she told me yeah, she guessed so, although just our dialogue had helped, too: the ritual of speech, some constancy in the night. It sort of grounded her. Did I know what she meant?

The plan now is to leave the club and head over to the West Hollywood motel where Chuck and the band, called The Hellionz, are staying. There, they intend to discuss Ann's idea for their album cover. I've just received this news from the drummer, Evan, who has the assignment of giving me a ride, since Ann has already met up with the others backstage. Evan and I are the only two left in the club. Nevertheless, it has taken him three approaches to convince himself I'm his man. I'm leaning back against the bar, wearing a blue blazer I bought specifically for a *Sports Illustrated* party earlier today, which makes me look as if I'm in the Secret Service. Evan is wearing a black undershirt and has his hair tied so that it points straight up, in a single frond. For the past few minutes I've been adjusting my cuffs, studying my grip on a soda glass, and Evan has been passing back and forth in front of me, like something in a shooting gallery.

Evan starts the engine in the rented four-door Chevette and then clicks it off again. "Look," he says uncomfortably, "do you mind if I smoke?"

He means a Marlboro. He smokes one all the way down, flicking the ashes out the window into the alleyway. It's a warm night, no snap in the air at all. One last deep drag and we're on our way. "The others won't let me smoke in the motel room," Evan says. "And Chuck tells me that if you get in an accident in California and the police find out you were smoking, your insurance won't cover you. It's insane. I smoke cigarettes; you'd think I was some kind of *fiend*." We ride over a bump and the top of his frond smashes up against the ceiling.

"He's pulling your leg," I say.

"Who?"

"Chuck. About the insurance laws."

Evan looks at me, and then he says, "Rock and roll isn't like it was. Nowadays it's people like Chuck. Nobody is straight with anybody else." He adjusts the rearview. "You used to know who you could trust by their music."

"I really don't know what the spirit of the joke was," I say.

Evan shrugs. "I take everything too seriously."

In the motel room, The Hellionz all frown over their drinks, lukewarm vodka and grapefruit juice in plastic bathroom cups. I volunteer to get some ice down the hall, bu Evan calls after me when I reach the machine, which I discover is padlocked. "You need—it's complicated." He isn't kidding. Beside the lock is a typed 5 x 7 index card headed, SUBJECT: ICE PRIVILEGES. "They make you borrow a key," Evan explains, steering me down a covered walkway to the front office. It's a 1960s-style motel, stairwell railings painted the colors of tropical fruit, and clean, but the windows are barred and there are hints of a new, bureaucratic embattlement; management cannot seem to invent house rules fast enough. At poolside, ten rules came with the preprinted sign, and two more have been added with a felt marker: *Number 11, Deposit Room Key to Use Pool Light,* and *Number 12, No Marco Polo.*

"I wonder if Marco Polo ever played Marco Polo," Chuck is joking, later. One eyebrow dances around. The "business session" has lasted ten minutes at most; Evan and I barely had time to pack the bathroom sink with ice. Now everyone has retired to the pool area.

Chuck is drunk. He lies on his back on a patch of lawn, calling out the names of constellations, a cup of vodka balanced on his solar plexus. When I walk by, he says hello without breaking his rhythm. "Pegasus, Capricorn, Ann's friend," he says. It's easy to see how Chuck's personality could get irritating, at least to Evan; but he has his charming side, too, if you're not relying on him to take anything seriously (and I'm not). By instinct he's a lovable drunk. If he says something sarcastic, he follows it by crossing his eyes at his drink, so that the joke is on him, too. Plus a repertoire of faces. The best is the one he wears to say he simply loves something; he shuts his eyes and smiles in a way that looks as if everybody is pouring champagne over his head. He loved Ann's cover concept that much, or he claimed to, which is how the meeting ended almost as soon as it began. One second Chuck's face was blank, looking at Ann's rough sketch (a visual pun, The Hellionz were tied together in a green bunch, like scallions); the next, it's raining champagne. I LOVE IT, Chuck roared, crouching in the middle of the room, eyes shut tight. Ann just looked over at me, dumbfounded, and mouthed a question: "What are we going to do now?"

What are we going to do now, in response to the fact that nobody has brought a bathing suit, is something that strikes Chuck as a priceless inspiration. We are going to play Marco Polo without the pool. Close your eyes, crawl on elbows, lunge at each other's whispers in the grass. What do we all think? Chuck scans the faces, beaming. That about does it for Evan; he gathers up his cigarettes and heads inside to write some postcards home. He asks how we all stand the level of intellect.

I don't know: personally I'm feeling relieved at Chuck's idea. I was worried that everyone was going to want to go skinny-dipping. I thought I was going to have to watch Ann stand there by the Coke machine and weigh the proposition, what it would mean if you were the only female and everyone was drunk and now you were taking off your clothes with The Hellionz. Thoughts like that. Not that Ann's behavior is any of my business. Weird that I should have to coach myself to remember something so fundamental. Things feel almost too alive tonight, neuralgic; the blades of grass superstitious and bare. I look at Ann, see a certain glow about her, and suddenly I could practically hate her for liking it as she might, the approval of these guys. Uncaring guys, fair-weather guys, guys she cannot possibly disappoint. I say this even though I've been like them before. Certainly I've been Chuck. I wonder what I resent.

And the resentment is so childish, I can only forgive myself for it, and the rest of them, too. I'm patting the grass with my palm now, just to feel it spring back; just to do something with my mood. Ann, meanwhile has declared herself "it." She hurls herself to the middle of the lawn, covers her eyes with her arm, begins counting backward from twenty, out loud, uncovers one eye. Even in that role, she's no child, exactly; she's a thirty-year-old woman playing a game—she shoots a reproving eye at all of us, as if to remind us of the fact. But there is an innocence to her just the same. An expression I've seen before. I'm looking up at the stars, remembering a time. We were at a concert and the lights had gone down and Ann went into a truly giddy act, started pretending the rush of camera fire in the arena was all for her. She was whipping her ponytail in it, skipping up the stairs in the colonnade. Lights popping all around her, a kind of lovesick sky.

She looks the same way now. Unfortunately, none of us has turned out to be terribly clear on how Marco Polo is played, with or without the pool. The result is that Ann is calling out "Marco," perched like a mantis, and the rest of us are shrugging uselessly at each other from opposite corners of the lawn. A long, awkward silence, and then, just as awkwardly, Chuck and I rush to fill it, chirping out *Po-lo* at exactly the same time, and with our voices in something too close to harmony. This paralyzes Ann. She tilts her head one way and the other, toward Chuck and toward me; then she just cracks up, flops on her side. End of game. Chuck yells foul, throws his plastic cup overhead; Ann wipes her eyes, basking in the lame coincidence. "That didn't count!" she laughs.

I go to bed still thinking about Ann's voice, which I've decided is extraordinary—the kind of voice I'd entertain myself with if it were mine; lie in the dark and test it, marvel at its honest weight in the room. Ann must know. She doesn't even mind hearing herself on tape, and a couple of times I've seen her play back my answering machine, intrigued. I can tell by watching her that she hears the same things I do, the layers. The young, scholastic quality, first off; the kid genius. Which must have been a curse to her at one point or another, the kind of thing grown-ups make a fuss over. Perhaps in response she has this other, worldlier tone, its own commentary, a voice that's a little tired of itself and yet more tired of trying to be anything different. It's the sober, lovely voice of a woman at the end of a day.

The month Ann left Seattle, I was asking Charla for a divorce. I drank a pint of Scotch to work up to the ceremony, sitting hunch-shouldered on a nicked piano bench. "I'm going to miss nights like this," I said. "You're wondering what I mean." The anesthetic had settle in and I was grinning and the scene deteriorated. Across the room, I watched my wife moving her lips. Gesticulating—like something under glass. Which I suppose was the effect I was after, though it horrifies me to look back.

Ann was working paste-up in the ad department of a Seattle indie record company, trusting her luck for the first time since her father died. She couldn't even name what had changed for her; she kept looking for something to thank. She strung a Casper kite overhead and named it McGhost. She was the first one at work every day. She liked everything about the job: the neatness of the work; the deft, styptic action of her wrists with an X-acto; the long hours on her feet (a good way around her big creative fear, which was Sitting Down to Work). Management gathered in doorways to watch her. The president gave her an office key.

Within a month the ax fell. Ann started using the key to steal typesetting supplies. This was fairly common in her field, but Ann didn't even try to cover it. When the boss caught on, she shrugged. She reminded him he was the founder of an "alternative label." He said she was fired, and absolutely without disrespect, Ann responded, No, you can't. Each thought the other was joking. By the time the whole thing ended, she'd made a scene. She tore down the kite and ran with it, she told me, a battered flight through the Seattle office, howling No.

For me that image holds a certain echo, a false déjà vu — as though I ought to be able to recall myself being there, playing some obvious role in Ann's life. Like memory, but with the carefully spooked air of a doctored photo. I'll see myself at the company picnics, or napping in a chair by her drawing board. I don't see myself at all when she's having her disaster at the record company, but I seem to see my absence; in fact, I'd swear by the look on her face that Ann is wondering where on earth I could be.

It's a short leap from all of this to My Theory — that Ann had been sending me extrasensory smoke signals across time — and around sundown I decide to get out of the apartment and go tell her about it. I expect she's in her studio with the stereo on, doing

The Hellionz design. But she doesn't come to the door when I arrive, and I don't hear music inside. There's that deadpan moment after an unanswered doorbell, the solid recognition of an obstacle. Our souls are one, but I missed you at home. I hear the dueling low dispute of a leaf blower far off with the whoosh of a car going by. It's a good sunset: Ann could be at the beach. I take a step back toward my car, and stop, because behind me Ann has opened the front door.

She wears stiff Levi's with a white T-shirt that shrunk too much in the shoulders and tugs at her bra; her hair is clipped back except for the bangs. She is all face, with brown bangs, looking at me as if a marginal joke has been told and she'll agree to laugh if I will. "Well?" she says. A broad smile going now. She means last night. I'm her reality check: she wants to know what I thought of it all. I'm following her upstairs, tossing her ponytail in my hand, and when I've taken too long to reply, she changes the question. What did I think of Chuck? This time I interrupt her and surprise myself. I kiss her square on the mouth.

And no sooner do I pull away than the separation feels unjust. Something stirs in me, solemn and fundamental. How long have I wanted Ann?

It's like this: When Ann tells me she slept with Chuck last night, I can't help it; I look away and jut my lip. This makes her ask what's wrong and I can't even tell her. I pretend there's a principle involved. I tell her Chuck is a creep; I tell her my opinion of her is damaged. Every name I think of to call Ann gives the thing more power instead of less, and when she tries to soothe me, it's worse. It was the mood, it was an impulse, it was "Berkeley," she says in the goddamn Ann voice and I run to the car, all her smart-neurotic protests following me downstairs.

So give me one night to get myself together. It's not as if we can't still be friends.

What's funny is the sounds you hear when you just stop thinking for a while. The Hellionz are on the turntable with the volume off, a flat midget screech living in the vinyl. Outside, I've got crickets, millions maybe — the backyard throbs — crouching beside their own dry ritual noise.

Ann says this all night to my phone machine: "Come on. Are you there?" Some static. "Oh man — I know someone's there."

After the Divorce

I NEVER KNEW HOW THINGS WERE RUN AND WHO mattered in the life of a town. How houses were built and sold. How children learned the meaning of a dollar. My parents failed to teach me though mom tried. Always with the story of the Depression and her pharmacist dad scared, and her rich thoughtless aunt buying her three dresses worth enough to buy a wardrobe, but they were all my mother owned for back to school. So she wore and washed them day one, two, and three, over and over from September to June.

I no longer think anyone can teach the meaning of a dollar. Practicality is an aptitude that people build on or abandon when they begin to see their trend in life. From the start my sisters were ambitious to succeed. Whereas I could never sustain ambition in the face of my mistrust. My Sunday afternoon father was a hedonist — as therapists have sometimes told me, I lacked a role model. When I was seven, a few days before my parents would surprise me with their divorce, he launched me down

Morrison Street on my bike, the great initiation, and let me fall while he went in the house stage-chuckling like a movie dad.

I was as lazy as an obsessive person can be (and vice versa). My obsession with work was to get done with it. I wanted a radar screen clear of threats. Responsibilities were enemy incursions and still are. And the liberty of childhood is sweeter living with a mom who is proud to struggle. You guard your fun like it's the only chance you'll have to turn out different.

Encino could be a sunny place to have fun, resembling countryside France burnished at sunset, or maybe the Midwest, the small-town parts where kids trade baseball cards and mailmen sleep in their trucks. Mornings were as foresty as a German fairy tale with gravel audible under tires at a distance of hundreds of yards. By noon, it was springtime. Shadeless blacktops, sprinklers, gum, bikinis, the radio. Until I was twelve or so looking at all this through auroras like a poet, knowing I would always be separate, knowing nothing could be sadder than the pursuit of fun, with its comedown, I couldn't bear it.

I labored under my grievance for half a summer without knowing that's what I was doing, reading comics by the pool, shooting baskets, and then one day started walking without knowing I was going to my father's house until I reached that point at the edge of a neighborhood where a walk becomes a journey. With all the sidewalks in Encino, you could still be the only person in town out on the street. Which ought to have made the moodiness of wandering more conspicuously pitiable than it did. More likely no one who knew me saw. One sister was grown up, the other was seventeen and too busy for me now, and mom was on the phone all day. The world was off doing father-son things, going to batting cages, or just lying on towels by their pools. Steve Breitenbach was at his aunt's in Culver City or with Lezlie Diever at Little League in the empty scorer's tower.

A few blocks up above Ventura Boulevard where Lanai forks, the thrill took hold that though it wasn't our day together I could ring my father's doorbell unannounced. The inspiration felt progressively more demented and real. Counting my way past all the mailboxes and gabled gates with my throat already dry. Trying to remember which house was the Jackson Five's. I was never going to be an Encino Hills kid or my father's son, but I could savor feeling left out and righteous. Though I was hoping he would be impressed in any case. The record would show that I'd made this walk, and it would be his choice to react, or stare at the evidence like a dope. He would see he was a weaker man in some sense than me, if I didn't cry or hold onto his arm or something worse. Even today, I can hold out as long as the sun is up for the story to have been about hope.

It wasn't my fault for loving him. Your father is a logical person to love, sharing somewhere the seed of your lack, and anyone would assume from photos that he was an easy man to hug, if not easy then at least inviting, because he was round, narrow-shouldered, wore his slacks above his navel like Jackie Gleason. Even his silvery stubble was soft and his cheeks had a lot of give. Watching sports on TV he half-smiled under his mustache as if someone he loved was talking over candlelight. He used to drive me home Sundays after taking me to a football game and pat the front of my knee goodbye and leave me in the driveway with the backboard my friends and I built together.

On that familiar ground my mom shot baskets in her red pantsuit. Evenings we'd play Yahtzee with her boyfriend and watch *Laugh-In.* She did her worrying late at night smoking in the kitchen with windows on three sides and a walnut tree in front of one of them—a gorgeous place to worry, the Encino flatlands. But the things she worried about seemed to miss every single point of what I thought the trouble was. If I was sad or my clothes fit badly, if girls never looked twice at me, it didn't bother my divorcée mom, only that I would never be a striver like my sisters. She thought it was the fault of my bitterness while I thought it was the way I was made. I wasn't handsome or brave. I was an unsightly wound if I didn't learn cleverly to cover the fact. Even my father cared enough to know that.

The straightaway part of Encino Hills Drive where the Lincolns and Cadillacs whooshed by had been paved and pedestrians forsaken. There was a series of side streets to the right that dropped down into gulleys so wooded there ought to have been streams. Then the streets rose again and circled behind the hill to some cul-de-sacs I wasn't familiar with. But the ground changed so little that walking could start to seem unpromising after all, with the air just as dry and the moment as neutral as when you started. Of course it wasn't the worst thing either, to have a long day in June just for walking, and even the inability to rise above the limitations of your life kept potential in the air, held you up for consideration of happiness.

With enough courage, a son could force a father's hand — asking, for instance, to live with him. He'd never offered, but when two men, or a man and his adolescent son, made a meal together in a kitchen, as we had done two or three times, the question was clearly alive.

The street where my father lived was at the top of the hill where the air cools and twenty-foot ivy-covered slopes climb to the lots of the homes, the asphalt darker as if it had been watered by groundskeepers. You could see some cute girls up there, Jewish ones in white hippie bellbottoms with hair like Ali McGraw in their Volvos and Beetles. My friends and I had been to a few parties on Calneva where the moms stayed home to party, moms who talked openly with the girls about life, sex, gynecologists. The dads were contractors who ate at Saul's Deli at 7 A.M. or earlier, a different breed entirely from my doctor dad whom I could have decoded if I'd had a chance to compare notes with him. I had no use for a dad like somebody else's, however happy and fit they might seem.

The houses went by with their slab Flintstone roofs. His was on a corner, painted in a minty green I had seen at the Otani Hotel, around the artificial waterfall where one of his stepsons married the former wife of one of the Dodgers. His refrigerator was the same color, and I can remember how it closed with a good hard seal, how it dispensed ice with a mineral odor, how the whole huge place was filled with conditioned air. The front door to the house was a double. He had looked softly interested standing there, not shocked or angry or even concerned, though he had to know my spontaneous arrival was an occasion, a development. He did say, "This is a surprise."

I drank three or four glasses of water standing in his kitchen wondering what it would be like not to stand and "visit," but instead to flop down in one of his stepsons' bedrooms like it was mine. Pass him in the halls without a word like families do. I would have hated the uptight neighborhood, but imagine the adultness, the emancipation, how your friends would come over and see you having a beer or playing poker with your father late some night. You'd grow six inches in a month. You would outsmart the fate of the lowlands where my mother smoked and worried. The dad who knew the manly secret of not worrying would never have to tell you anything — he'd never even have to like you. He'd be your North Star, and you would see how, without trying, you would grow to your inheritance, as two points make a map.

The question is, why didn't I tell him? Now that I knew what I had come for. I can't swear he'd have rejected me again. It's just that all the answers I could picture coming from him were embarrassed avoidances. Conveniently he might say that he had wanted me early on, but now we all had to adapt to the way things were, after the split. Brute indifference is more bearable than this kind of consolation, which assumes you are too fragile to insult. Questioning a father's love is a lapse even Jesus could never expunge. So I told my father that I just happened to be out walking. Then I accepted his friendly offer of a ride down the hill.

We got there quickly, and unlike his neighborhood there were kids playing football in the street and stores you could walk to, guys you could knock around with to make forts out of scrap, and I always did feel more at home here, if never quite as free as my friends seemed to me. It was one of the only times he walked me to the door. For a golden interval my parents and I stood in the entry, the two of them marveling about my ambitious hike, though if they had talked about punishing me it would have been almost as fine. And I memorized the closeness between their bodies, never touching but in close enough range that their companionable words barely rose above whispers, yet with the best of manners as they inched toward good-bye as if from a hospital room that was mine with a long night ahead.

I went forth to have a pretty rocky life after that, failing at money and marriage but blessed with good kids. My mom took forever to die from emphysema, but my father went painlessly from cancer. Invited to his home toward the end for one holiday or another I stayed in the shadows, making toasts with my troubled step-sister-in-law, the once-famous Dodger wife. By then he was divorced a second time. My sisters and I inherited an insurance policy from the navy that he may well have forgotten he had. Everything else, he gave to a girl-friend.

Signal Hill

BACK IN THE '80S, WHEN LIFE WAS GOING WELL enough, Richard Leviton almost fell in love on account of a woman's laugh, and also her tan, both of which looking back contained hints she might be crazy. She was a bright divorced mother from Wisconsin with a high, desperate laugh, the kind that actresses in melodramas used to have just seconds before it gave way to sobbing. The tan was an L.A. newcomer's magnum opus. It had no lines at all, years before tanning beds, the insensate red-brown of a naturist or a girl from a Deadhead Gathering.

He saw her whole tan one night after a fund-raiser lunch that she had helped publicize for the presidential campaign of Jerry Brown. The Brown organization in Los Angeles was chaotic enough to involve someone like Jaimie Gorski in a position of serious responsibility. Leviton had been a depressed reporter with an idea of being a fashionable under-achiever. These were his twenties, when he felt thrown into the professional world with all the seams of his middle-class upbringing on view. He had been compensating for his insecurity by drinking, and with a juvenile approach to picking up women at parties that suggested they had stolen a car together and driven it across five states.

He watched Gorski revel in the camaraderie of the luncheon, sprinting from one best friend to another in the crowded dining hall. A record heat wave didn't slow her down, and in the days before the fund-raiser, when it was clear that there was something unspokenly damaged in common about the two of them, she walked Leviton around Koreatown during lunch breaks, stopping to drink Gatorade with vodka under a tree outside an acupuncturist's bungalow, happily answering the questions Leviton should have been putting to the candidate. Her skirt looked thin across her knees, and her anxious laugh made its impression, something like a premonition of Gorski unprotected, or trying too late to hide a hand of cards. On this scent of feminine jeopardy, Leviton was so aroused that any flattery from his lips would temporarily have been true. He could have proposed to her there on the lawn. Instead he just told her to kiss him (it came out halfway like a question), and she did— first gathered herself up to this new turn of events, then closed her eyes and gave him her whole open mouth, as if she were both disappointed and utterly used to this.

After an obscene kissing spell in the parking lot at the fund-raiser, Leviton followed Gorski to her Topanga Canyon guest house. Her son, a kindergartner, was still in Madison then; she had moved in bringing only her clothes. Husklike leaves littered the side streets in early evening sunlight so flagrant that Leviton could count acorns along the sidewalks and gutters. Some surfers and a general-store disability crowd at the corner tiptoed through bottle glass. Behind the clapboard main house was the courtyard garden, laboratory of her tan. There was a splintered gazebo and a gourd of vodka by a lawn chair on a towel caked with dirt. The scene was as primitive and fresh with her absence as a shirt hung on a nail. This was her fuck-you to Wisconsin.

In the middle of the night Leviton lowered himself onto the lawn chair, no longer in love. Gorski lay hot as a sauna rock indoors, all the windows open and a bottle of aspirin in her fist. He'd had to hear about her childhood. She told him she'd played Queen Esther in a Bible musical, dressed in veils, turquoise baubles, and a floral tiara, and that afterward a relative molested her. Using Leviton's hand to demonstrate, she literally hissed more details. Leviton grew shy. Not that her confession was so threatening per se, or even so novel to him in the psychic unveiling room of sex. But she was cathartic about it, getting nervier and more talkative as Leviton shrank. Her husband was the last man before Leviton, and he had broken her jaw.

Leviton's unease with Jaimie Gorski helped him justify giving up the Jerry Brown assignment, and he never wrote to her or phoned her back. Yet when she dropped him a line, he felt an egotistical lift, and he hoped that she would flatter him for a while, keep on writing, until she understood that the interest was one-sided.

II.

Leviton was big, and he could be generous, especially on his own turf, never prouder than when counseling someone else, squeezing a pal's shoulder like he'd seen his own father do. He toted a beer bottle and grinned like the young Charlton Heston. He counseled and grinned and all of a sudden it would seem to him that he'd been ridiculously out of line. Then he'd grill everyone who'd listen: *Was I — you know — butting in?* He'd married young and divorced by twenty-three, assuring his partner that their problems had not been her fault. But his humility was as convenient as his generosity. Suddenly single, he threw a summer solstice party, hiked to the Griffith Observatory every day, and got drunk at lots of Dodger games, leaning over the left field rail to scoop a fistful of the red clay warning track. He ate beans and rice at about a thousand music benefits, where he would be carried away by the miracle of belonging: to L.A., his times, and his friends. Love letters were instant souvenirs from what Leviton already regarded as the legend of his twenties. He didn't know what he was memorializing the years toward.

Gorski sent him three letters that summer. The first one drew him erotically into the violence of her divorce. "I pretend you were there, washing my bruises with whiskey and rags with your lips almost touching my lips, asking me if the blow was as bad as it looked. I say, 'No worse than a Goose Gossage fastball.' Our ribs touching when I say that . . . and you kiss me. (Oh Lordy.) Rick-eeeeeee! Yer lovin' makes me strong. I've always been a clown when I got hurt. Like a puppet shot from a cannon. I asked for it, you know. No, you don't know."

In her second letter, Gorski said she regretted that she had never showed him her second bathroom. "The bathroom is the quirky feature of the house from when it was a canyon clinic," she wrote. "It has a window tray for cups of pee with no lab on the other side. Whatever used to be the lab was removed. (Or slid away?) There's just an excavation that smells like sagebrush. You can find old '50s bottlecaps in it if you dig a quarter of an inch with your thumb. I found a Bireley's Orange Soda and a Squirt. Is all of California like this? You dudes are crazy."

That was the letter he might have been tempted to answer, but her next one scared him out of it. "I'm a shut-in since Friday (fading and peeling!) because the fog rolled in like a carpet. You had to see this to believe it, creeping right up to my towel, like next it would bite me on the nose. It's seriously cold too, Northern Calif.-like, and not the treatment for a mandibular fracture. I walk and the whole left side of my face rings. PLEASE don't let it be winter.

"Here is a secret, but it's a bad secret. You're going to turn on me when you hear it. Things keep materializing from my childhood. The other day, the pee box was left open a crack, so I closed it, only it was painted shut before (!) and my necklace from 1969 skittered to the back of it. So help me god. That wasn't the first time exactly — there had been other things I found outside in the garden, not just bottlecaps, but this toy holster with rubies on it (my mom once told me the scabs on my shins were rubies, and I believed her — and then my brother tore them off, and I still believed her), and a rose petal lollipop of a kind you used to see everywhere. You can suppose these things were from whoever lived here before (and I live atop a mass grave for all you know), but I know Harlan. And Harlan would not be above trying to drive me crazy. Which someone is not above, when someone thinks they're going to be God. Do you know Mormons? Harlan is Mormon now. While I am the Priestess of Malibu.

"Right now the plaster around the drawer gives way like papier mâché, and I doubt any dampness in the air could have done that. Though I will admit I don't know ocean fog like you do. Either God wants to set me over the edge or Harlan does, and I'm not going over any edges anyway, hear? I'm not even scared — I just feel like poor Harlan, poor me, and that's all, poor all of us. It's not like I can't absorb a little pain. If you know me one bit, you know that. You should try it sometime, really, when all your supports are 2,000 miles away, which is a unique relief. You find out you can't be destroyed (or gotten rid of — whoop-de-do). Except that I feel like I'm standing knee-deep now in regrets and everything pretty I assumed I would grow up to be and never did. I just might happen to feel a few things over this.

"This is your last free letter. I could hurt you but I won't. You tried to look so macho with your cigarette in the morning when the whole reason I opened up to you in the first place was that you were shy. And you have a ridiculous face. A long droopy Jewish face. The Brown workers made fun of you every day. You make love like a girl, and that's if I get you going enough to make you feel equal. But I was an injured birdie, wasn't I? You were what I needed, the next best thing to a man. Want to hit me? I'll still always know. Cheers—Jaimie."

III.

The marvel was how Leviton inventoried the memory of Jaimie Gorski. He wasn't wounded by her ridicule—if anything it moved him that she had been so provoked—but he was appropriately repelled, an instinct that enabled him to keep the thought of their sexual drama at a remove from which it could thrill but not threaten him. It had the integrity of an adventure whose ending has been foreseen, like the reminiscence of a spouse who has died, and Leviton continued to think of Gorski on and off, right through middle age, always at moments of stress. He thought of her when his mother died in Granada Hills, outliving by two years an oncologist's prognosis and her own goodbyes until she gave up trying to die, shoved past her live-in nurse and dropped dead by the door to her carport. It wasn't known where she'd intended to go. When he got the news, Leviton walked straight to a liquor store and smoked his first and only cigarette in a decade. One for the '90s. But at the point of inhale came the memory of Jaimie Gorski's lower back—an oven to the touch, an image that pacified him for days. Maybe all the sadness of modern life could be dissolved by something that brutally carnal.

He mixed her up with places and feelings. Pain was a reliable trigger. A toothache or a muscle pull would seem to invert to another reality altogether, a universe he understood to be home to Gorski's injured jaw—primitive, antediluvian, the turquoise Pacific materializing with the tide of his breath.

At those moments Leviton took Gorski to be a vaguely romantic, if dark, angel of recuperation— the goddess of the coast and the germ of a bag lady— knowing full well that the actual Gorski was trouble, someone to be avoided. As he set his feet on the floor in the morning, he rarely felt as bleak or as forsaken as Gorski sounded in her letters, but if ever he did, he felt this outsider past was there, offering company.

IV.

Then everything started to go south. He had a golden beard and a kindly gaze by middle age that was not a bad shortcut for the most part to feeling kindly, although it backfired on all three women he'd married, each accusing him of smugness just when he felt he had triumphed over selfishness the most. He had been an occasional actor (several small theater productions, one lucrative airline commercial) and, wading beyond his depth, correspondent for a local public radio newsmagazine. He had an eclecticism rooted in compassion, his journalism tapping a closet boyhood empathy for scapegoats and playground pariahs, for Richard Nixon trying to rap with protesters on the White House lawn. He meant to peel the covers off hypocrisy. He began a story about feminist reporters intimidating the newsroom ("anti-woman," they'd branded one of Leviton's commentaries, a good one, folksy and skeptical with lots of male bafflement in his inflection), taping a station manager's protests to use as quotes. Editors begged him: "Richard, how can we use this?" Crushing Leviton freshly each time.

He knew, that is, that he was drifting. But he maintained the deliberate fantasy of melting all opposition by being so truly himself. Instead there came his veering-off years, Los Angeles of youthful inspiration disappearing in a rearview mirror, its druggy starlets, all the ghost-filled canyons and groves. It was a credit to Leviton or his fear of freefalling that he hung on for years where he fell. He landed (by marriage) in Lakewood, a suburb near Long Beach, fathered and divorced, resented his unromantic neighbors — who did not recognize his sensitivity, or even much notice him really — and sold plant stands made from bar stools, downsizing his dreams, a nightschool workshop having spawned a midlife career.

He spent lunch hours at the gym, Long Beach women everywhere, and his own image interposed in a wall-length mirror. Leviton and every kind of girl, a sort of musical burlesque. His favorite, a striking young Armenian with a trace of pudge about her middle, struggled up the Stairmaster every weekday, lighting up the room like a visitor among the inmates. Sundays, there was Kids' Klub (calisthenics optional), where Leviton's five-year-old son Zachary lay reading on his back, leg crossed over bent knee like Groucho Marx. Leviton and the last wife had succeeded this much in the incubation of self-esteem, the world was the child's Barca-lounger. Eventually he'd get beaten up at school for sheer arrogance. One day by the stationary bikes, Leviton turned to ask a weathered man who wore a yarmulke, "Do you think I should make him take karate?" And the stranger said, "Well, where's the good in forcing him? You risk losing his trust. Suppose one day he gets his nose broken in karate—"

"No, no. That's what I'm worried about if he *doesn't* do karate."

The stranger looked like he was going to argue and then made a big show of learning not to over-step himself. "All I can tell you is that's not my experience. I know what you're saying. But it's not my experience."

"Are prayers answered?" Zachary once asked him tearfully, and then prayed never to die of thirst. Once, after his boy went to sleep, Leviton prayed, like a child himself, to be rescued from drudgery—

to be blindfolded in his track suit, spun, and pointed in a providential direction, a prayer he'd reasoned could not go unanswered. What kind of God would brush off such simple consent? Discerning no definite reply, he tried to assume he'd been led to where he was, a Lakewood tract.

"It looks like amateur porn without the sex!" the wife of a visiting friend exclaimed.

V.

A mortuary secretary, whose staid femininity Leviton fantasized as risqué, told him days before the funeral, "The rabbi's honorarium will be $350." Leviton smirked—so this was religion. Quietly he announced he'd find a rabbi himself. He walked outside, never feeling more intensely like a knucklehead, but valiant: a mother's son.

His only lead, as it happened, was the stranger from the gym. Miraculously, the man claimed to be a rabbi (a Jew for Jesus, and his congregation was on the Internet, but no one had to know). Even more miraculously, he consented to preside. If he hadn't been available, that was going to be tough. Something told Leviton: You're really on your own now. This is adulthood.

Leviton remembered the service as a series of agonizing visuals. From an ancient Dodge Colt the rabbi emerged in pinstripes, laborious and hunched, as though he were being ordered indoors by someone taller. He withdrew a folder of notes from what looked like an old physician's bag and posed stock-still, awaiting the wonder of speech. The moment lingered, and lingered—*was he drunk?*—and Leviton thought he saw the lectern tipping forward, à la Chevy Chase's old pratfall as President Ford. It was a false alarm, the 23rd Psalm. The eulogy talked about the prodigal son, dwelling disastrously upon the word *inheritance*— "accepting the inheritance that is yours," the rabbi clarified, but mouths had already begun to drop. He then swept his arm across the room, a gesture meant to encompass the miracle of the universe, and Leviton's eye followed outside to a parking lot that was hot, cropping with dead weeds, and almost lurid with motorcycle exhaust— a scene of pure unfiltered fallibility. A couple from another funeral was doing a turnabout in a green sport utility vehicle, and right then Leviton decided to spend half his inheritance on a green sport utility vehicle. It was hard to define why, or why now. He had seen green sport utilities before, he had seen happy couples driving them, but he had never enter-tained the notion that by buying the same car, he might impersonate their lives. At this instant there were no limits on Leviton, no scripts to follow. He could have conned his way into a medical practice or kept two wives in separate towns.

On Friday Leviton drove to Signal Hill Motors. Raising dust before the rows of unibody cars, his small camper-shell truck, which he'd liked just fine up until now, brought an atmosphere of time travel. A salesman, pomaded and buffed, swept at his face with a handkerchief in the spring heat. The ceremony looked soulful, the grief of the California breadwinner. "Rodney Dangerfield," Leviton said out loud.

"It's an honor?"

"No, I mean he does that with the handkerchief when he performs. Throwing out one joke after another. Like he's trying to sell bow ties from a trunk."

"'Aaaah, I get no respect,'" the salesman recited, without enthusiasm.

"No respect! I never even realized I liked him," Leviton added. To one side he had already glimpsed the SUV, forest green, an almost criminal heartbeat passing. He disguised the feeling, lingering instead at the sticker on a sport wagon.

"This has a thousand-dollar rebate," the salesman said. "Do you camp?"

"I chauffeur a few kids sometimes."

The interior was in a nylon-and-neon motif, with the word "Sport" painted here and there in a jetting sort of hand. Some moldings and rises and visual confetti reminded Leviton of a woman's running shoe. He climbed in, stepped on the clutch and pushed the shifter around—supple, a tumble of rubber mallets—wondering just how long it would take him to make an invention of such newness feel worn out. Dissolve the rubber of its construction like an enzyme. Everything that fascinated Leviton about the armor of possession also shamed him, things he couldn't even mention without sounding like a desperado: the hiss of climate control, the whir of economy.

Even more so with the SUV, when he drove it— its command, its muscular poise, like the leaders and realtors who populated Leviton's town. He imagined vacationing with a new girlfriend, a dental hygienist or a supermarket checker, unhooking her bra in the vanity of a motel. They would make a random turnabout in the driveway of a mortuary, skis strapped to the roof, as the sales brochure depicted it, and the back would be filled with his plant stands, along with an array of pristine, never-used sand toys. He argued a thousand dollars off the price—an advantage the salesman theatrically conceded, then nullified by writing up the contract as rebate-included.

While his electronic keys were being programmed, Leviton took a flight of stairs to the customer lounge. A showroom window extended to the second floor, from where he could see the flashing air-control beacon at the top of Signal Hill. A teenage boy was squatting before the view and talking to somebody Leviton could not see. "I don't get the light. It's not like there's any buildings to protect." From behind a desk labeled MARKETING, a woman's voice said: "Yeah, just waste those airplanes, then." Leviton thought he recognized the laugh.

Inside he saw Jaimie Gorski's nameplate and then her face, involuntarily hopped, and almost said, "Yikes!"

"You know, I recognized you on the lot," Gorski smiled, shaking his hand up and down once like a cartoon pal.

She was a little less tan now but still reminded Leviton of an oddball—something disturbing about her sundress, as though it might be secondhand. Her squint was deeper and her mouth sagged like a small water bomb. In an oxidized mirror, she might have looked regal. "I was going to come looking for you. We were just having a deep discussion about air traffic. Peter has just said something timelessly stupid. Just to show no acorn falls far from the tree."

Her son gave an art-student kind of handshake and returned to squatting by a shelf of CDs. He was slender but almost bell-shaped in the middle, as if six months ago he might have been fat. He had a receded chin on which he was stroking a revolutionary's patch of goatee.

"You both—live here too?" Leviton asked.

"It's too strange to be funny. You two never met, right? Peter was in Wisconsin with his father when I came west. His girlfriend sits like that—" She corked her thumb at the squatting boy. "They eat dinner that way together, without chairs."

Peter Gorski hummed something that sounded to Leviton like: "And ever will."

"Here's the truth, Richard," she said. "In fifteen years, anybody can wind up anywhere. What was it you told me about San Diego, Peter? My geology scholar. In a million years, San Diego will have dropped off the coast of Alaska. Why shouldn't the world be a little—unhitched? I was going to say unscrewed. Screwed is not a reversible condition. That is another world you can't escape."

"That's interesting," Leviton said. "Because I just bought a car I never imagined myself buying."

"He knew you would."

"Who, the salesman?"

"Yessir."

"The salesman?"

"He's very good."

"I guess he is, if you're not kidding."

"It's all over the office," said Gorski. "You had to have the bride magnet. Do you have any clue how much money you lost not bumping into me first? What did you trade in?"

"Oh, I'm keeping that, too. A Toyota truck."

He'd forgotten to ask someone to drive it home for him, though. With an inward sigh he knew he did not trust Gorski enough even to confess this dumb mistake.

The boy tossed a series of paper wads at a wastebasket and then walked to retrieve the misses—an unfluid, lopsided walk, as if he were pulling a rickshaw. "He has an SUV?" he said suddenly.

"*Oh, Christ, don't,* Peter. Can't Daryn's stepdad help you?"

"He's got a load of bricks in the truckbed. And also he believes it's illegal. It's just a five-minute drive."

"They're scavenging tiles and wood for an art project," Gorski told Leviton. "I already ordered Zanhkou chicken. You could eat with us if you're staying around."

Leviton checked his watch pointlessly.

"C'mon, man," Peter Gorski smiled as if it were a comedian's trademark line, or the name of a game show, which an audience would shout in unison. *"Are you in—or not?"*

"Not?" Leviton joked, but with a shrug started downstairs after the boy, who had committed himself to walking as if on his own ludicrous dare. He was snapping fingers at both hips. Conceivably he had never led anyone down a hallway on a secret mission in his life.

Leviton beheld, as if from the wrong side of a tectonic event, this process of events as it detached him from his better sense. Yet as soon as the paralysis began, it felt familiar — a childlike urge to be swept up and conveyed by forces beyond himself. All at once the three were outside, with a PA system squawking overhead.

"Peter will point you to the house. You're a good sport, Richard. What, did you think only girls are good sports?"

Leviton searched himself. The spring air was beginning to cool just slightly and a dolphin logo on the dealership sign porpoised against a chalky sky. The San Gabriel Mountains were visible to the north across a quarry pit of towns.

"The things I wrote about you were so true," Jaimie Gorski said to Leviton's amazement as the new car pulled away.

VI.

It began in the newspaper time and flared up with fatherhood, Leviton's awareness that he secretly, almost narcissistically, wanted to do something good, live more truly or (it was horrible to express) look like certain people who he thought *looked* like they lived truly, store clerks, coffee-shop hostesses, men on their breaks outside the barber college in downtown Long Beach; a train porter in Montana he met who read jokes to passengers from *Reader's Digest;* the drug-addicted guitarist Keith Richards of the Rolling Stones; all monks of one kind or another, or in the rock star's case a proud mistake. It was a scoutlike ambition to become Loyal to Himself, to be a person whose hair on the last day would fall the way God had arranged it when he floated in the womb. But he worried, being a reflexive worrier, that it might already be too late for simplicity, that people might be inseparable from the personalities they created through decades of cowardice and self-betrayal. Leviton became more apprehensive of his direction when the last marriage failed and when seeing his face in an airline commercial not only stopped bringing pleasure but left him with lonely disgust.

Leviton didn't mean goodness in the sense of doing charitable acts to stop being bad. He meant it in the romantic sense of being the person he would be if he stopped worrying for himself altogether—if he could get up the courage to have his life be reclaimed by whatever was indivisible within him, and who could? If he didn't have courage it only meant he really didn't want it enough. But he envied the courage of saints, the faith that his own willingness to be a fool for his soul would guide him and provide for all his needs, or else his needs weren't worth talking about in the sight of the ages. It was an impulse that lived in everybody deep down, but it seemed so unmodern now, like the atmosphere of a sunken city. His capacity to be spontaneous nowadays meant being superstitiously available to people who asked him for favors—and, as an embarrassing but not completely unrelated exercise, smiling when he answered the phone. A popular book told him it would change things from within. Though he always felt ridiculous doing so.

He liked Peter Gorski from the first, in an uncomfortable way—half wanting to protect him from his awkwardness and half aware that it was awkwardness he loved. They had driven for five minutes in amiable silence while Peter gave directions. The errand was to collect some bits of decorative tilework off the leveled stairwell of an old ranch house that fronted a Chevron discovery well. A cyclone fence around the demolition was well trampled, and the KEEP OUT signs looked perfunctory.

"If you see a piece with most of a rosette painted on it, we really really need those," Peter said importantly, digging in the damp dirt layered with foxtails. " 'Course, most people don't throw them out." He blew sharply onto a chunk of black or cobalt blue ceramic and the dust didn't even move. He gripped it with a snapper, twisting the tile back and forth and attempting to scissor it. He was perspiring. "What am I trimming them here for? Let's just scoop up what we see."

The intact stuff had been salvaged by the corporation and the remainder was throwaway "scrap," or someone named Daryn had told Peter so: It would be useful for some school projects the two students had going, and for a magnificent surprise Peter was making that Daryn didn't know about yet.

Afterward Peter Gorski gave directions up the hill and sang inaudibly along with the radio. "Nothing in this folky music is new, I hope you realize," Leviton said.

"It's all about the girl groups now. They have all the soul."

"Nobody can have 'all the soul.'" Though as soon as Leviton said this he realized he wasn't sure about the general trend, and the boy squared to face him.

"Okay, tell me a guy could do this. I asked Daryn to the Wedge with me alone, and she hugged me and said, well, it sounds like a date, and I haven't really felt ready to date again since Bryan. So the answer's no. And then not even another word about it. She doesn't hold your hand or stare into your eyes like she has to make sure you'll survive. A guy cannot do that."

"I thought she was your girlfriend."

"She's my friend. My best friend."

"What did you do?"

Peter Gorski laughed, his goatee stretching. "I flopped backward on the grass and I told her she was my idol. She said she hoped I was making fun of her." At once he became a little teary. "Do you believe in handwriting analysis?"

"Do I believe in it? Not only do I believe in it, I don't know a thing about it."

"They should analyze hers. Look at this, but absolutely positively don't read it." He pulled from his pocket a canary-colored page and refolded it into eighths before Leviton could make out word one.

"You have to wait till I park if you really expect me to be able to tell anything about it."

"No. I shouldn't have shown it at all."

"It's that personal?"

They reached the Gorski home, a two-story garage unit no larger than a carriage house. There they settled on bar stools in the kitchen to wait for Jaimie Gorski to arrive with the chicken. "Okay, here's a tiny line." Peter Gorski had creased the paper into a brick around the phrase *Love ya, Daryn.* "What does the shape of the Y mean?"

"She has a long lifeline?" Leviton said. The writing looked as sovereign as any sample would, its rotund D like a boy's attempt to monogram the snow. It was an industrious signature that was loaded with shaky slipknots and the ink was impersonally black. "I guess I find it encouraging somehow that girls still pass notes to their boyfriends."

"I told you, she's not my girlfriend," said Peter Gorski.

"How did you become best friends?"

A sigh. "She chose me as her partner in Diversity to make these mosaic gifts, which I call Hebrew Hotplates. And she started sending me notes addressed to Late Bloomer, because I'm seventeen without a license, and telling me to always be true to myself. Which is not something she would say to Bryan, incidentally. Who broke up with her, but he still shows me the notes she sent him, and one of them was all sophisticated, 'Sorry I've been a bitch about writing.' I'm like, excuse me? 'A bitch about writing'? Because no one had ever heard Daryn curse. No one even liked her until Bryan did. She was this Jewish honors student with posters of Buckminster Fuller who takes math classes at UCLA, and she's graduating early, and then all of a sudden they were walking from the bus real solemn and she had her arms sort of thrown around his neck and shoulders. Which is way up here for her.

"But that note to Bryan sort of got to me. I was lying awake reading it over and over, thinking, this is someone I thought I knew better, but my heart's just pounding." He folded his arms and his voice was sturdier. "Basically she knows that I love her. But we're agreeing to be these great friends instead. I feel like it's the most amazing thing you can do. But I know not one of my friends would approve of what I'm saying. My Diversity teacher says I will have my pick of women someday for developing my feminine side."

Leviton asked to see the magnificent surprise, which was upside down in the garage, four tall posts poking upward as its mosaic underside was swabbed with grout. It was their mutual dumb luck that Leviton actually knew what a huppah was. He had been married under one of these long ago. He knew there were supposed to be four posts and a canopy, and as far as he knew the canopy was always cloth. As far as he knew he had never been married under the frame of an iron TV stand with an inlaid mural of tile and grout.

Architecturally Leviton had some real concerns. As a play for a girl, it was about as astonishing as anything in human history, although Peter Gorski insisted it wasn't about that — Daryn could file her nails for all he cared, and angels would serenade her as they serenaded Eve, for whom God fashioned ten huppahs made of gems and gold, said the Kabballah. Leviton thought of his own son's confusion toward a kindergarten classmate, who told him how she was going to marry some other boy. "You can marry him," Zack Leviton told the girl, "and I'll marry you."

In the mural, ghostly bearded faces shimmered together like flame tips. There were pyramids and a myrtle tree, with shadows falling in all the wrong places. It could have been child's art or a Camel cigarette billboard.

Jaimie Gorski had no love for the creation. She arrived in the carport with twin bags of food and turned fast on her heels. "Did you put in a word for common sense, Richard?"

"It's pretty majestic," Leviton said.

"Tell his bride to wear a hard hat."

VII.

The first lights came up from the Long Beach harbor though it wasn't yet dark. Leviton and Jaimie Gorski sat while she talked about her job. She had remained a person who smoked while she ate. Across the room was an adolescent encampment: lank Daryn and Peter and two other boys who had refused a ride from Peter's mom. They had hiked up the hill to squat at the edge of a sofa, passing chunks of crystallized ginger from a satchel. There was candlelight and in its shine Leviton noticed Gorski was wearing nylons, a new feature for her, and rouged cheeks, which reminded Leviton of the faultline of her jaw, and her hair had gray roots, cosmetic desperation pitted against age. Cutting his chicken and having learned almost nothing ever in his life, Leviton felt attracted. He glanced away as if for help and became aware that someone in the room was being teased. Helping at the preschool had given him a sixth sense for the inspirations of mobs. Peter Gorski was trying to smile with the others but was met by a synchronized silence. "You don't know what's funny," Daryn said and her open palm jolted his shoulder.

"What the hell are you mad at *me* for?"

The two other boys bounced outside to the porch where Leviton lost sight of them. "Whose suburban assault vehicle?" one of them said.

"I don't deserve to know what's wrong?" Peter Gorski asked Daryn.

"Peter, come here please." Jaimie Gorski searched his eyes. "You're *letting* them. You don't need this."

"Mom."

"Ignore her. I can drive us all to get Richard's truck."

Daryn spoke up. "It's just that every time I don't go with you, you get the wrong tiles. It's like you don't listen. Typical man," she added for Jaimie's benefit.

"I didn't even know you were mad about that," Peter said. "All you have to do is tell me."

She picked at a chicken bone.

"You know that, Dar. We can make another haul," and all eyes looked at Leviton.

This time the kids led the way on a dirt trail, hands in pockets, their Pendleton shirtbacks descending the slope like plaid sandwich boards. Leviton's vehicle followed behind because he wouldn't have remembered where to go. It had not occurred to him that all four could have fit inside. Gingerly he drove over ruts, afraid of squashing anybody. Aside from the SUV, Leviton felt almost like one of the gang.

Trees were stirring and footsteps thudded on the wet dirt. An occasional oil well was penned by pipe rails. Beyond a clearing Leviton's tires rolled onto Temple Avenue from out of the muck. He parked in the same slot by the trampled fence but saw the teenagers go over a second fence within the property, the springy chain links eddying under their boots.

A quiet minute went by. Two Hefty trash liners rolled over the top of the fence to Daryn and a Filipino boy, who turned back toward the car with their stash. Leviton was watching Peter Gorski through the fence. He looked like a still life, smiling, dreamy, too dreamy, too still, and behind him, simultaneously, everything changed. Either the barking came first or a shadow sense of the dog Leviton registered now sharing the picture, rounding the building, as if sprung from a trap.

Leviton yelled. The dog turned toward Peter Gorski who caved into himself with his crowbar bouncing away. He buried himself in the fence, and the taller boy had the crowbar then and he was backhanding it at the animal full force. You could not hear it strike, the dog was on it, and now the dog had the crowbar in its jaws, but the boy was free and Leviton made out a dog yelp of distress. Both boys scrambled safely over the fencing before Leviton had gotten ten feet from the car. "Shit!" the taller kid was yelling, again and again and didn't care how loud, pacing in tight circles and feeling for his face. The taller boy fell upon his friends, a hero's welcome. Peter Gorski was stooped for breath and Daryn was behind him.

Leviton kept asking if anyone was hurt.

"Was it something like being out of your body?" he heard Daryn saying a moment later. "What were you thinking about?"

Peter Gorski laughed and tried to lean on her but instead of her shoulder he met her eyes searching for his.

"If it were me, I think I'd still be holding my crowbar," she said. "They'd have to pry my fingers from it at the hospital. Did you thank Russell for rescuing you?"

"Russ, I owe you, bud," Peter Gorski said.

"How does someone drop the only thing he's got to protect themself with?" Daryn said.

"I don't know."

"If you don't know, I don't," she kept on. "That's why I just asked what you were thinking."

The Filipino boy was grinning. "No joke, he's like covering his ears with his wrists, dude, what is that?"

"I didn't say I was an animal tamer," Peter Gorski halfway smiled.

"Talk like yourself," Daryn said, dragging the trash liner over the dirt and past Leviton's car. "Why am I even talking about this?"

"Use the car," Peter Gorski said. "Your bag's gonna get heavy up the hill."

"No, Peter, look." Her eyes seemed past pretending. "Maybe I need to feel how heavy my own freaking bag is."

"Look, is everybody all right? Do you need me to phone someone?" Leviton asked.

Peter Gorski said, "Daryn and I need to talk for a minute."

Daryn was already up the trail.

"I'm going with her, I guess," Peter Gorski informed Leviton.

"No!" Daryn shouted from ahead.

That was all Leviton saw for a while. Peter Gorski trailed the others, not really trying to gain ground. Where the trail joined the road Leviton pulled ahead and waited. Peter Gorski still pleaded with Daryn to talk. "Why won't you come here?"

"No reason." Her answers tested the waters of shamelessness. "Because you're a pansy. Pansy, why are you following me, pansy?"

All Peter Gorski could say was, "I'm just *walking*. I have to walk, too."

Then Leviton recognized the lidded clack of a dropped tile or two and as the group approached the Gorski driveway he made out Daryn deliberately chucking one piece at a time down the road and Peter Gorski scrambling for each one, the group egging her on, until she swung the whole bag around her head emptying its contents into the ravine, setting the boy into shrieks.

That did it for Leviton. He backed up alongside Peter Gorski with the passenger door open and reached for him, polo-style. The others ran laughing and astonished down the hill. "Forget the damn tiles," Leviton said. "You can't find them in the dark."

"If you shined your lights!" Peter Gorski was nearly sobbing.

VIII.

They stayed parked, Leviton trying to construe himself as a helpful presence. It was a curse to second-guess your own usefulness, maybe even a sin. What you wanted in crisis was to be a freak of self-confidence, a southern preacher, an old-school man with the heart to risk being lampooned. "Son," he would intone.

Or glow with tender tough-guy wisdom, like Hollywood actors did lately. It was the era for male circumspection (could men be at fault for that too?), and Leviton had not come easily to it, nor to adulthood itself. He considered it a triumph that he had taught himself to pave a driveway and keep a lawn. He lived in a community and nothing was communal. No ancestral prototype prepared him for that.

He felt too the persistence of an old, vast superstition, the same one that moved him to leave the dealership with Jaimie and Peter Gorski: the sense that unexpected duty could be freedom in disguise, liberation, our savior in the clothing of a beggar. A realization of hope, sized precisely to their mutual insufficiency, would take hold in the cabin of the truck. So Leviton imagined. "Aren't we even going to do anything?" the boy asked.

Leviton quoted the basketball coach John Wooden ("Don't confuse activity with progress"), then felt pompous.

"Don't make it sound so zen. If you just aren't up to the hassle."

"I'm not up to crawling around in a ravine and getting frustrated. And dirty," Leviton added.

"They're far now. I can't even see them. Could you see which way they turned?"

"No."

"God *damn* it."

"You really could let it rest," Leviton said. "You could try to."

"Why does that air conditioner keep hissing?"

"It's a climate-control thing. I don't know."

"What a joke." Peter Gorski flicked the back of his hand against his closed window. "Who buys something like this? They're out there and we're in here. It's too sad."

"My other car is a camper van," Leviton tried to joke.

"Twice a year my dad visits from Utah in his Mercedes. He drops me at school and everyone stares."

"Look, there's nothing wrong with spending

your money." Leviton felt defensive now. "As long as you know you're all right without it."

"You don't get it. What's wrong is someone else's money. And pleasing my dad when I don't like him."

"Well, that's a luxury problem," Leviton said, "if I've ever heard one." He only felt more irrelevant now.

"Mom will help me," Peter Gorski said, and left the car.

Following him inside, Leviton heard but did not see Jaimie Gorski erupt. It was a sick-sounding fury, batting at demons, as if a son like Peter, at a moment like this, were the symbol of her punishment in life. *"Can't I just once enjoy a visit with a friend?"* she screamed. *"I have had it with your idiotic project. Had it!"* The boy called her a name, Psycho, and Leviton glimpsed Jaimie running through a hallway, heard a door slam, and another door, heard uninhibited sobbing.

Leviton ducked through the kitchen to the garage and sat himself someplace on the cool concrete. He wondered if he should say something reassuring, like, "Well, it's a full moon, everyone's bonkers today. Look at me! I just bought a green SUV with smoked windows." Or, "We knew we weren't going to catch up on fourteen years in a single evening." The shelter of the dark garage was profound, and the feel of his hand roaming over a carton of tile chips brought back a childhood of captive wanderlust — days when a bolt on the road or a found chunk of clay could seem like a remnant of forever. He remembered, straight from the heart, a homemade carnival that he erected when he was seven. He did it because his older sister and a crowd of her friends were staging their own carnival down the block, with tents and games, and even a go-cart straddling a rail. In a bold stroke of counter promotion, Leviton's carnival opened the same day, to no customers and with a broken-off pole to which he imagined he might attach a tether and a ball. But he could not pack dirt tightly enough around the base of the pole to support it. So he leaned it against a tree, waiting for the rest of his carnival to come to life. And at moments, from certain angles, it actually did, the Marvelous Tetherball Attraction standing tall on the rusted mouth of its steel pole, but toppling when he sent a ball circling around it. He remembered the sound of felled pipe on the earth.

This huppah, Leviton thought, isn't too bad. He had seen clumsier things installed in galleries as art. The rabbinical figures were awkward, but awkward in a way that nudged you to consider the odds, as if they'd pieced themselves together from the most preposterous hardships. There was a fashionable patina to the iron, and the tilework was opulent, though Leviton didn't know if the opulence it reminded him of was Judiaca-ancient or only California-ancient, from the utopian days before California was all aftermath, if the aftermath wasn't built in from the start.

The noise had stopped, and in a moment it was Peter who reappeared to apologize. Leviton clapped him on the shoulder and the boy stayed around an extra second. He had promised his mother her parking space back. If it wasn't too much additional trouble, he hoped to stand the huppah on its legs. Each wielding an opposite post, Leviton and Peter Gorski teamed forward to raise it, two marines on Iwo Jima.

The last cup of coffee with Jaimie Gorski was for courtesy only. Leviton intended to ponder the strange day that had passed, and he intended to ponder it from on top of his own bed, in the amplified calm of a party's end. But when he felt for his keys, he realized that he'd left them in his new car. He looked across the porch; the car was gone.

Peter Gorski failed to answer when they called.

With this realization came an explosion — a literal explosion, the Friday night fireworks from the *Queen Mary,* and Leviton was seriously rattled now, as though in his existential waywardness he'd touched off a land mine, or an antimatter universe. He ran behind Jaimie Gorski's silhouette under crackling skies to the bend where Daryn had flung tiles across the ravine, but halfway there, Leviton knew the boy was past considering a return to the scene, aside from there being no glow from a headlight for miles.

It made slightly more sense that Peter Gorski had driven to Daryn's, or someplace else meaningful to him. But whatever the boy's holy places were, Jaimie Gorski had not been let in on their location.

Friends were called, and then hospitals, and at four in the morning Gorski reluctantly called the police, who moved squeaky-soled around her kitchen with their holsters grinding into their waists. Someone also reached Harlan Gorski in Utah already leaving for work, but he had heard nothing in weeks from Peter, who in any event could not reach Salt Lake City before lunchtime even if he had money for the gas.

Finally, Leviton was a refugee, heading to the dealership before light, and it could be miles; he had no idea how many blocks he and Peter had glided past on the drive twelve hours before, reprogrammed to walk now. He nearly welcomed the catastrophe, an excuse to kick a can, rethink life. He reached absently for a cigarette, as if that addiction had never left him. He walked for fifteen minutes and let hope rise at each four-way stop of seeing Peter Gorski stranded. When that didn't happen, Leviton considered that his predicament might be serious, and false hope retreated to the borders of night vision: He was alone. Yet Peter could not be all that far away, and a lot could go wrong from the thief's point of view, with highway patrols and spike strips and the imperatives of money and gas. He might crawl the car into a landslide basin, confusing the accelerator for the brake. Or spend half a day trying to hack open a can of spaghetti with the keys to Leviton's SUV. And break down right there and then: He was not pioneer stock. He struck Leviton as soft, a little eerie, the hesitation of his smile and his head tilted abstractly, his gosling, newborn listening like the marveling of the blind.

IX.

It took a week to recover the car. Leviton was trying to work up the proper sympathies for Jaimie
Gorski and failed to call, a lapse that made him feel
like an errant child himself. Not that she'd been the
model of contrition in Leviton's life either. But she
kept his answering machine informed, cell-phone
messages that crackled in and out of range like
occult transmissions. When a postcard from Peter
assured her that he was fine and informed her where
the vehicle was (in Joshua Tree National Monument, keys and license plates buried beneath an
information kiosk), she supplied a Mexican valet
from the dealership to ferry Leviton to the site.
They made an unimpressive repo party, Leviton
thought, chasing Gorski's trail into the desert, and
probably rubbing it out as they went. He stayed on
with Zachary at the Hot Wells Inn, which despite
its name had a lawn like a private golf course,
spending $850 to experience the desert for three
nights in the style of a credit-card ad.

Back home, Leviton blinked once at his sur-
roundings, as if he'd never seen his living room in
daylight; then he reentered life as a loner. This time
a loner with an SUV. The last wife had left him the
place, as if to say: *Happy?* For that reason he had not
let it become the anticipated dump. When Zachary
was away, however, the decor hung suspended in
irrelevance. Wednesdays and weekends the boy
dragged a canvas bag containing Pokemon cards
and clothes over the floor heater in the hallway to

his bed. For Show and Tell the children in his class were assigned to describe Something That Tells Who I Am. Zachary chose as his topic My Bag.

Winter nights, Leviton slurped cereal straddling the heater, postponing sleep, which he loved, though not the family-less kind. Moving his computer to the bedroom, he masturbated to pictures of the Web's Youngest Women, downloading models in cheerleader outfits to folders according to hair color, then dragging them to the desktop trash, ashamed, after his tweezed, prophylactic orgasm. To sleep on a sea of noncontention.

Leviton's wife had been a child star, and she had the heartsick charm of a clown. At fifteen, she made a joke that was bleeped on the *David Letterman Show.* ("Life's been . . . a bowl of popped cherries, David.") Leviton loved her the way men love only once in their life, but having been loved that way since puberty, she wanted none of it. He did love her True Being too, and the way that her clumsy beauty unnerved her, although he might never have looked for True Being if she weren't all that beautiful, and he was imprisoned by the guilty cliché. His most altruistic affections aroused him. She resented him for his need, and he sulked in their garage, sketching love acts in a secret notepad. Marriage was a comedy of injustice.

To Leviton's bathroom mirror was taped a lamination of the Prayer of St. Francis of Assissi ("For it is by self-forgetting that one finds . . . by forgiving that one is forgiven . . ."). He used to recite it as he shaved in the morning, but he had stopped seeing the meaning behind the words. What he did see in the mirror one day was a cowlick, a dorky one, and felt ashamed, so he razored it down. He carved and carved until nothing sprouted there at all, not a bump—surprising, how many passes it took—and the shorter section of hair sifted back into place just like wild rice. The accomplishment gave Leviton a feeling of deftness, justice, and pleasure. He became a compulsive haircutter in that moment. He carved some more along the side of his head toward the front, admiring as he went, turning this way and that, for the briefest moment mystified as to why Hollywood had never made him a major star. For who else, Charlton Heston notwithstanding, looked quite like Leviton? And with a knack for hairstyling besides. And with a grasp of the casual accident: boyish, Dionysian, a crown of leaves. Leviton strode whistling from the bathroom to change into a fresh T-shirt, the old one having been sprinkled with gray-blond shavings, then returned to the mirror, razor in hand, but the light fell differently on his work. Somebody had anvil-stamped the whole back of his head, and he looked like a mental patient. Above his ears, pale bulk billowed forward. He ignored the ringing of a phone. Possibly, he reasoned (don't panic now), he could recapture the texture of the first accidental stroke of the blade. And possibly not, he didn't know. What he did was rework his haircut from scratch, but only made it worse, scaring himself now. It served him right. So he would live with bad hair! A week of humility, maybe a month. But turning to leave the bathroom Leviton looked back, his silhouette askew, and felt his throat narrow, just exactly the way his throat used to narrow when a director ruined his best scene in a play, and right there, standing before his mirror, Leviton kicked a gash in the door of his vanity, how well it was named.

He gave a clenched shout-groan, bent over with his hands on his knees, straightened himself up, and returned to cutting his hair. Two nights passed in search of the cut that would make Leviton's hairstyle rhyme. Finally in the act of lashing out at his son for interrupting, he caught sight of himself. This time he all but fell upon the words taped to the mirror. His need felt second-rate to anything Francis could have envisioned when he recorded his great prayer, yet here it was, on a laminated card, in Leviton's bathroom, of all places. The saint, he imagined, could not now retract it.

At the gym the rabbi called to him, pointing with two fingers in the way that basketball players acknowledge a teammate for a pass. Leviton never knew if that was to begin or to bypass conversation. He took the adjacent bike, their wheels humming like propeller craft. "Okay, well, I ran six miles one time," the rabbi said. The rabbi often began conversations in the middle. Was six miles a hardship? A personal best? Leviton fumbled to answer, but the rabbi continued, "When I got home, I had forgotten my key."

A long pause. A possibly final long pause.

"Well," said Leviton, shaking his head, "how did you finally—"

"Then my wife answered the door, just out of the shower. Her robe was not tied, her hair was half dry." A breath of garlic escaped from the rabbi, or possibly gin, and he turned a childlike face to Leviton and asked urgently: "Is there anything more beautiful than a woman in a robe? I'm serious. All of fashion is put to shame by a woman in a robe, who is clean and warm and—" His eyes went poetic. "Shampoo-scented! And thirty-two years old. Which is young enough to play a schoolgirl on TV, for God's sake, but it's also old enough for a body to have its, its—its candor, Richard, its *authority*." The word pleased him greatly. "Oh, it's springtime, Richard."

"I'm a dirty old divorced guy now," Leviton volunteered, his eyes parenthesizing the roomful of femininity. "To women, I'm a fencepost."

The rabbi swept a lock of hair behind his ear and said, "You should try the yarmulke look." The rabbi was very buoyant today. "Consider yourself lucky. One of them gave you a son. No one knows why they do it! You're not Harrison Ford."

Leviton wanted to reply that he had been to parties with Harrison Ford. "We gave each other that son."

"What is your son, six? You could be ready for another one."

Leviton pulled his teeth into his telephone-answering smile. "Have you heard nothing that I said?"

"I know that surely there is a purpose for you."

"And you know that, because there are so many lovesick old men in the Torah."

"Well they were around, obviously."

"Obviously," Leviton agreed. "The cockroaches of history."

"Not at all. They were among the leaders and the mystics. David was a lustful king. He had a man killed so he could sleep with Bathsheba."

"Lovely name. I'm not trying to argue," Leviton said, but slipped in his last word anyway. "You can just feel like you're taking up space. Inheriting money and buying things, pleasing yourself." This came out morose.

"I feel lots of things. Youth is over when it's over. Why were you in such a hurry to be mature? You should have postponed it. You should have been an old blues singer with nylon socks up to his knees and racy women draped over him. It was a mistake to get reflective so young. Look, you're an artisan." The rabbi had plenty of ideas. "Art will keep you in a full head of hair. Those tables you make will out-last you. So will good works. That goes without saying. Right? Right?"

The rabbi waved good-bye and Leviton bore down to contemplate all his errors in life. In the wall-length mirror he saw himself pedaling: Big face, sweatpants hiked high, a scowl to scare Beethoven. He glanced at a television and saw coverage of a strong-man competition. Contestants carrying concrete luggage stumbled toward a finish line. They called this extreme sport and its whole ethos was about indignity. Leviton's indignity was that hardly anybody valued what he valued about himself at forty-four, which was that he knew a thing or two, knew enough for instance not to be arrogant, which knowledge made him a crank or a loser to the young. Also, he had survived more than once being brokenhearted, a boast that bored him almost as much as it would bore a younger man hearing it, and maybe he was not really better at all for having lived through being hurt if nothing could hurt or reach him again quite like the past.

Whereas youth was ever entitled to its pain. The young women at the gym, especially, made it look like such hard work to be children, and Leviton prayed they never got to where it looked easy, because then they would have outgrown the mantle of complaint and someone else would be beautiful and young. In the aerobics room they step-aerobi- cized, hip-hop girls flinging their massive breasts. He was lucky to be alive in a generation where all the young women worked out and were in wonder- ful shape. The drawback was that they were less variable in their beauty. Except the Armenian girl. With her pudding of flesh at the waist and her sullen clomp. Of course everyone on the Stairmaster clomped, but the Armenian girl clomped more poignantly, Leviton felt, and she missed whole steps outright, as though she had been left behind by a brigade of older friends. Lately she smiled when Leviton saw her and he would pull his lips into the businessman's smile of his airline commercial. He knew that she worked at the library desk, and he thought once or twice that she had recognized him there. She had smiled at any rate. The plateau of understanding that he had hoped to attain by midlife would have told him whether the smiles of younger women meant that he had come into his own or whether he had passed into spectral harmlessness. Her hair seemed a fragrant tumble. He imagined it blown half dry and her robe unsashed. He imagined her pale olive breasts, as outlandish in daylight as rubber doves. He pedaled harder on the bike and looked up with his airline-commercial smile but she wasn't on her machine anymore.

He was driving home with the sunroof opened and the road coursing beneath the floorboards uneasily so that he felt in his knees the danger that even a low-speed collision would present. But that collision never came and neither did a single traffic light turn red. Nor did the car need to be steered for two miles more until the street would appear that was his own. This suburban linearity felt not like joy but like deprivation, and for the first time in his life he felt oppressed by the promise of more summers than he had seemed to plan for. He felt as nauseous with desire as an immortal, and more so on account of the new car, which made him eligible for the kinds of junkets and flings that he felt were a young man's to take. Lakewood refused to resist him or even impose upon him a pedestrian for whom to stop, and when he did see from his window something that once might have aroused his literary curiosity, like an Asian housewife or an overgrown lawn beyond a mysterious gate, it slipped by him with the rest of the scene, backdrop to the green phantom that he drove. He knew that an afternoon's work would outlast this feeling and deliver him to some other mood, and he would enjoy running the soaked cheeseblock sponge over the enamel of another plant stand; for the restlessness of his mood was only the same restlessness he'd had when he was twenty years younger. But youth's restlessness had made him feel that anything could happen, whereas in middle age it shouted like a car alarm that in the wake of a theft was the one thing that had failed to be disabled.

After a tuna sandwich he showered and imagined his muscles absorbing the protein. He pulled on a fresh pair of army twill slacks and a fresh T-shirt that was clean but splattered with paint. When he undid the padlock to his garage to begin his work, he felt a shadow approach and heard the collapse of shock absorbers and saw a big sled of a car pitch forward onto his driveway. The driver was a teenage girl with greasy black hair. The passenger was Daryn. But she no longer had hair. The driver placed a kiss between the cords of Daryn's shaved neck. Daryn got out and stood before Leviton and looked in his eyes. "I know, I look twelve." The car she came in tooted its horn twice and drove away and they were left standing there alone.

She coughed a seal's bark. She did not look twelve but gloomy and sinuous like a prisoner of war. On her dog chain was a Star of David. "I kept trying to ask Jaimie about Peter but she kept telling me you would know."

Leviton's bewilderment was plain.

"All right," Daryn said. "I knew something was off when she said it."

"I just can't imagine what she meant telling you that," Leviton said cautiously. "He wrote to her that he's okay."

"Oh my god," Daryn said. "And she wouldn't tell me. Oh, you got your car!"

"He arranged to leave it for me. But he wasn't in it."

"Jaimie hates me. I mean, Peter hates me too, but he'll forgive me."

Leviton glared at that assumption.

"I don't mean it like he'll forgive me because I'm so great. I mean that he's a totally different person than she is." She lit a clove cigarette as Leviton watched. She threw out the match and offered a soldierly hand. Leviton shook it.

"I just want to say I'm sorry about your car, and pulling all that stuff as if you weren't there."

"Oh, you didn't steal my car."

"Yeah, but also, I don't know how to say this, but I don't normally behave that way, either. Peter didn't just look for some lowlife person at school and decide to be her friend."

"Right, he did say that. He admired you." Leviton had been unsure about saying that.

"You'd have to have known us to understand. I had talked to my stepdad, and he said Peter shouldn't be friends with me if he's in love with me. And I saw how I was upsetting him and that he wouldn't fight back or defend himself. You know, Tolstoy says every cruelty is planned by nature. It's how bees trim the hive. Have you ever felt like you just were going to take the blame for something no matter what you did? I have never done anything like that. Never! But someone was going to hurt Peter sometime and all of a sudden it was me. And then I felt like I just had to. I mean, Jesus — grow a scar or something. My bio-dad left me and moved to Israel, but if I just laid there and cried nobody ever felt sorry for me. Get up, you know? Get up and do something."

"Well," Leviton said. "He did."

"Yeah. That's true."

Daryn rubbed her scalp and began to cry. "But I liked myself better a year ago."

"Listen," Leviton said, shielding his eyes from the sun. He was going to say nothing and even thought it would be best, but there she was with a tear running her cheek and he felt philosophy rising, felt against his wishes the old Leviton. "I'm probably not the one to know. Or maybe I am. I was the kind of kid who had to understand everyone. And it could be just that you and Peter are basically sensitive, smart people, and it's partly a curse. Not to sound pretentious. But I was this perfect student, and then I ruined it all, I think because I needed to see what I was capable of. I would judge some group of people who I thought were cruel, and then all of a sudden I'd see the integrity they were after, and then I'd try on their postures and their convictions and then I'd see it go bad. You have the disease of openness." He was swollen by compassion. "But you can't go wrong, you know? How can you go wrong? You're on the path. You're on the great quest."

"No, stop," she said. "You already said it. It's so

wise. I was meant to hear this. Can I please have a drink of water? I'm glad I came here today."

Leviton led her inside. Daryn marched in looking lost, like one of those juvenile guests on a daytime talk show. (Moms Ask Daughters: Why Won't You Dress Like a Lady?) She drank the water and wiped her mouth. Her presence felt slightly unrecommended now. A tattoo of what looked like a cactus flower rose up above her belt.

"How did Jaimie seem?" Leviton asked her.

"I don't know. She looks like a drag queen sometimes. Sorry. She made me help put the huppah out in the yard. It was sunset and I saw the sun come up on it the next day before school, and the ground looked all shrubby and matted underneath it and you can see the oil derricks through the posts. Now everyone sees it on the way to school. Like London Bridge that got moved to Arizona. Everyone talks about how Peter wanted to marry me."

"How did they even know that was what it was?"

Daryn didn't answer.

"You told them," Leviton said.

"Well," she said, "now I feel very ashamed. Maybe that's what he wanted me to feel like. I've disappointed you too. And you're looking at me like he looked at me."

"No, no. He loves you."

"But you're staring at me," she repeated. "You're so intense."

"Oh, stop. I'm a father—I've *loved*," he reminded her. He lorded the word. "You and Peter just make me remember what I was like, at one time or other."

They were still standing by Leviton's sink.

"I'm embarrassed," she said. "It was an ugly thing to do. I'm going to make mistakes, just like you said. I was being the school celebrity." She released all her air. "Why can't I even look at you without feeling like you know everything I'm going to say?"

Leviton fidgeted, too flattered.

(Mistily:) "You really are a good person. So wise."

"Well, now. Maybe you invite what's good in someone," he said.

"Oh, but that's true, isn't it? I get what I look for. The divine in me salutes the divine in you. Namaste. That's what the word means."

"Okay. Namaste," he repeated.

But she seemed hypnotized by her own noble sentiment and he knew that she was leaning in to hug him, implacably, so you couldn't tell if it was a spiritual gesture or insane. Then all at once she was crying in his chest. Her breath close to his face and her denuded head was like a greyhound's.

"Thank you," she said. The hug was fast and perilous. He patted her. His hands avoided her tattoos and swept over her flanks.

She stepped back and then pressed her warmth upon him once more tightly and quickly.

Leviton shut his eyes. He looked both ransacked and furious. "See?" she said, comprehending. "You're phony, too."

"Lay off," Leviton begged. "What can you know about what people mean to be?"

"Oh, you were acting all generous."

"Don't act so shocked by life. That's the worst thing about a young girl."

"I'm not shocked. I do appreciate your kindness," she said. "You're a good heart. I think you're very cool, okay?"

"No," Leviton choked, "but you can trust me that you're fine. I mean — you're beautiful. Regardless of shaving your head, or whatever you think you have to atone for —" It was becoming a near-drug experience for Leviton, with inspiration and hormones reactivated, set loose like that bull from the malt liquor commercial.

"You know what?" She pressed her lips against his temple. "I'm not into men. But I can see why girls sleep with men who say nice things. Oh, this feels so wrong. I have to *go*," she whined, as if he had her by both wrists. "This will be my number in Westwood, if you hear anything."

She left then with staged breathlessness and a crooked smile, bumping into door frames, and Leviton was sure they both hated themselves, having made springtime seem to stir because they could.

X.

He remembered a time in Austria on a travel assignment. Leviton had left the Hotel Tyrol with no agenda, and that was his agenda, to walk and keep going until he found the feeling that fortune had welled up and taken hold of him, like a tarot card migrating to the top of a deck. He sleepwalked through town squares and Christmas vendors, waiting for the rest of his life to begin. In half an hour he had found his way to an Austrian stag party. Leviton was engaged to the third wife at this time; the idea that his first Austrian outing had led him unerringly to a nudie bar was not without chagrin. Not to mention the suspicion that his experiment in spiritual communion had been a crock; that he'd both detected the migration of his card of fortune and planted it; that outside his impulses might lie nothing unspoiled by his shadow, Leviton in the theater of the usual desires.

Yet there at the metal door to the speakeasy, in a half-second's trance of innocence, he felt promise, a bliss approaching motherlove, as though he'd happened upon a lesser-known Catholic charity, a topless one, ministering to the lonely travel writer. He would later see that his route had carved a rectangle through the city with the storefront in the final block of his return. He could have got there from his hotel by taking ten strides backwards.

German porn movies were playing in what seemed to be a gallery space, pigtailed girls on the screen thrashing atop their lovers and chanting Americanisms. Waitresses performed on a makeshift runway and some of them were for rent. To prolong his guilty prospects Leviton overspent on cocktails, deliberating over a bare-breasted blond with black German features and rabbit teeth and brassy nipples, spending so much that he finally could not afford the trip to the back room. The personnel had just possibly seen his kind before; for some odd reason no one helped him budget. He'd have been out in five minutes had he known what he wanted. But it was his ambivalence that inflamed him, and comprised the girl's power and appeal. She was six-foot-two when she rose half-amused to do her show. She was the best of the waitresses and she starred in an improvisational sex act, which was called Bride of Solomon for reasons not entirely faithful to Scripture. The idea was for an adolescent-looking shepherd-groom to channel love psalms while pleasuring her, an invocation the Divine was obliged to honor despite the cheesy trappings. This schoolboy blasphemy both thrilled and appalled Leviton. He could not judge from his limited German if the poetry was inspired, but he saw with his own eyes (or imagined?) that the sex was. He could only suppose that the performers had learned to confuse themselves nightly into the feints of passion. Toward crescendo came a filmed backdrop of flora, Georgia O'Keeffe—style: jungles of origami. Then it had ended, lights up loud on paneled walls and acoustic-tiled ceiling, to reveal an actor in briefs defiling a rose. Leviton would wonder a decade later if he'd dreamed the whole episode. But he doubted that a dream could feel as four-walled and arid as what he'd seen.

He was making so few plant stands now. Perhaps he was too much of an artist deep down to run a business. Perhaps the rabbi was right about the sanity of being a father and building plant stands and doing good works. And thank god for work! Thank god for hanging around the Seal Beach nursery, for buzzing bees, for small talk with the proprietor, his client. Could that be enough? Whenever he lived not for the sake of how things would turn out, but for what he guessed could be called the Zen of his life, he felt all right, with less fear of age or obsolescence. Ironically, these rituals of duty felt not only more important than the product of his labor, or even the success he could produce in his son, but more tangible—when he went to bed at night, when he swept a beacon over the landscape of his day, they were the only croppings of rock and clay that caught the light and glowed and formed shadows any longer: a human connection, an apology, a nice try.

But there was a panic accompanying this recognition, as if the rocks themselves were signposts to a no-man's-land, lost from the reassurances of the physical world. They pointed to ancient caves, braceleted the graves of pets. What was he supposed to do with his desires? What about Leviton the lover, David the lustful king? Why did he have longings if not to act on them, make messes, live large?

Sometimes in Lakewood, Leviton just seemed to drive from one stop to another, ending at his gym as often as not, as if he had never penetrated the backdrop of the town or the toy gaze of mountains, and with the suspicious feeling that he was not even a citizen of the life of his town, only a fly on the map of it. In Bellflower were surplus stores and a shoe emporium and a boulevard of what had to be more than a dozen churches interrupted by baseball diamonds and parks. Signal Hill was the only elevation at all on the Long Beach side of San Pedro, and around certain curves it could look like the Hollywood Hills, but only just enough like the Hollywood Hills to break Leviton's heart—something about the Cuban light, and the ruins of appliances, which in Hollywood had been the mark of profligate bachelorhood rather than of rifle-bearing parents who drank. From the car he saw Peter Gorski's huppah in front of Jamie's house looking archaeological, just as Daryn had described it, alongside a torn padded bar chair that Leviton fleetingly thought he might use for his work. The desertedness of the scene brought back the improbability of that dinner with Peter and Jaimie—they might be on different continents just now that had been one continent accidentally for one day. Nor could he find again the mouth of the foot trail where Peter and his friends had left Jaimie's house to scavenge for tiles, leading Leviton into their deeper wooded nation.

What he saw all that summer were bedrolls. The desk at the gym posted a warning to gatecrashers who had been using the place to take showers. Leviton once saw a trio of sleeping bags heaped outside the emergency exit. The stack smelled like patchouli and other people's hair, mixed with daybreak, something that had sage in it, a memory of clothes hung from lines. The fact that Leviton never saw the perpetrators made him feel poignantly slow, and a little irrelevant, as if he were a news anchor who was always late arriving to the scene.

The same shampoo scent seemed to linger in his garage as he worked—was it dust? Was that how garage dust smelled to someone whose entire sense of hope was blown back across old associations of summer and linens and morning? The fragrance became undetectable when he searched more closely for a source. Once, Leviton kicked something along the floor of his garage that proved to be a tippler top for a cup of coffee not his own, tossed from a speeding car maybe, sleeted in apparently on the wind with a rim of dry leaves, and this tiny encroachment of his workshop upset him, not that he'd ever been so fussy, but it implied that a certain backtide was against him, that the world was just a closed, potentially stagnant pond, like the environmental posters from Zack's kindergarten class had it—something to that effect, with Band-Aids on a blue-and-green mass of papier mâché.

There had been home invasions all over, the papers said. On TV toward the end of August Leviton would see film of one victim, a young Jew addressing media questions on her lawn in Granada Hills, eerily mastering her role at the nest of microphones to discuss the assault. It struck Leviton that she looked like Bill Clinton's mistress, the intern, with the same regality, that tilt of the chin—*rising to the president's demand!*—as if (and the president must have seen this at one exquisite moment himself) her mistress-ness were her victory and not his. He thought the victim's name was somebody Gold and in her eyes there was that booby-prize celebrity, the inheritance of the world's fame just when the world has up and left. Then the media ran out of questions and, in a profuse, ending gaffe, the woman thanked them—*for what?* Flustered all at once, she marched away.

XI.

"It's all about the girl bands now," Peter Gorski remarked to the owner of a flat-roofed roadhouse called The Back Road in Twenty-Nine Palms.

The lead singer wore a hunted gaze stabbing through the spotlight as though she were practicing to burn herself into the memory of her assailant. She said she'd written the next song, called "The Shout," to a girl who became a varsity football player at a middle school in the Pacific Northwest. The title referred to the shout in this football player's head as she learned to hit and tackle. The singer's voice was wary and cool and reminded Peter of fresh skin beneath a bandage. He thought about how natural righteousness must be for women. Their lives were a conclave of healing and self-care. Panties swaddled the cosmic wound.

"You would have thought the nightclub came first, then the web site," the owner said, across a picnic table lacquered in the oil of fish and chips. "It makes no sense, I know."

"I don't know. It makes a funny kind of sense."

"It's just that there's a sense of tradition about it. The club, I could tear down and build someplace else if I wanted to. It was never going to be anything but a set for the live feeds. Till we had all these ringers here applauding the acts and I thought, shit, I'm *paying* them? Why not charge them for the beer? Whereas the live stripper page has always been home base. I want people to feel like they know the place when they land there. It's got to maintain a constant . . . feng shui. It's a red-light cathedral by modern standards. That's just how I want it—Click to Choose Your Girl. Maybe show a row of dressing-room doors." He made some notes on a napkin. "Not to cramp your style," he sighed. "You draw better than I do. The dating classifieds, you could go hog-wild on. And I want an advice column, and a request line for the high rollers. You'll have to fake some requests to start. Some of these people couldn't match a bored housewife with a pool man."

He handwrote the word *Casting* and underscored it. "We've had it with the stiletto blonde Hooter Girls. I want you to think Junior College here. Latinas, Cambodians. Look for the sort of girls who line up to scream for Celine Dion at Tower Records. Ones you'll meet in school. They're unspoiled and they're a little insecure. And they're caught between their future and their parents. You see I'm a story man at heart. I'll give you ten thousand dollars!" He leaned back and waggled an imaginary cigar. "Ten thousand free and clear to send me a girl who just wants to be an American! Well, five hundred, anyway. Probably that's just my story. *I'm* the fucking immigrant."

"Do I bus tables and set up there too?"

"How about if no one else can help it." He seemed disappointed by the question. "Figure it out for yourself. You squeeze oranges like you're putting your hand into a shark tank. I wish I'd snapped a picture."

Peter Gorski looked embarrassed.

"Don't you worry though. I have a good feeling. Do you know you look a little Middle Eastern? I saw it right off. Intelligent forehead. Sensitive. Dumbfuck American wouldn't know it if a juice machine bit his arm off at the elbow."

Lucy, the headlining stripper, walked over and kissed the owner on the head. "Tuesday at the Wilmington club," she said.

The sun rose obscenely hot when Peter rode with her to Wilmington near Long Beach. Because of a swollen wisdom tooth, he refused breakfast and lunch, substituting root beer floats, pitching the nerve of pain under a snow of fulfillment. The car was her boyfriend's collectible Plymouth with a steering wheel as thin as an iron halo that she held with both hands like an applicant for a license to drive. She had on a Danskin under jeans, very Hooters. Peter felt vaguely anemic, skeletal beside her. He could feel the surface of the inflamed molar, as seared as the flat rocks of the desert. Earth was a wonderland of pain.

He had reached the desert two days earlier in panic, slept in a cave, then huddled himself in the eye of the emotional storm. The SUV by daylight was as bright as a model kitchen and had on its console an appointment book filled with faux notations

("Big Presentation at Sotheby / Call Ed in Phoenix").
A marketing prop. He didn't dare sleep in the car lest
somebody arrest him. He climbed a rock with a tribe
of kids at a campground and found his balance right
in the middle of being wobbly, as if by giving in to
danger he had learned a way to rhyme the vibrations
of his fear. Rappelling afterward, he saw he was
covered with bruises and cuts. The rock had been a
vague, flat sensation outside the chamber of his calm.
That night he hiked miles to the highway, saw the
neon sign blazing GIRLS, a blue flame of identity.

"What video were you in?" Lucy shouted over
the din. There was no air conditioning. Hot wind
battered the interior.

"I wasn't in anything," he assured her.

"I thought you might be that guy with the thick
glasses—the weird kid who gets his mind blown
by Bambi Morrison or Chelsea Hunt. There's a
whole series about him."

"No, I go to school. I'm graduating a year early.
If I can clear a couple of things up," he added.

This would only solidify her impression. With a
look of fatigue she dropped the subject. "Massoud
seems to think highly of you."

"He said I could have been him when he came to
America."

"Maybe you are the heir to the throne." A cyni-
cal stress on "throne."

"Well then I couldn't be the next him. Because
nothing was given to him."

Lucy speculated, "Most of us just hated our dads
and chose weird friends."

Together they drove like sightseers. He basked in the look of her—the swollen, depilatoried lewdness, and the athletic suggestion of her outfit, as if she'd been employed to play volleyball in heels. Nevertheless he felt untortured by attraction. It was pure sensation and, as he'd discovered in five strobe-lit nights at the club, nothing that needed to be named. All he wanted now was to protect what he had gained on his rock climb in the desert—fidelity, a filament of himself—and there was no explaining a thing like that to anybody, but he felt the implicit acceptance of these loners in his life. If now and then he felt sad, lonely for his mother or the diversion of old friends, he cast his attention instead to this project of inward consent.

In the back of the Wilmington club was a gym where the boyfriend was. Lucy smoked in a doorway and waved to him.

"That's the guy you have live sex with on the web site?" Peter let himself feel half-mad for her again.

"You keep waiting for the perfect time to stop," she explained. "But eventually it looks like you're never going to get a sign, or you figure you don't deserve a sign. I really think there is a certain calling about it. I always looked oversexed, which I used to hate. My mom used to say, Don't stand like that! You know what I think? I'm a public icon. I'm made to be laid—not by *you*. But don't you think there's such a thing?"

"Hey man," said the boyfriend, whose shirt read Big Game James.

She climbed in back.

When the car reached Lakewood, she said, "We're all getting where we have to go. This is the losers' bracket."

"Drive past without slowing down," Peter Gorski said, checking the address on a vehicle registration. "I'm staying in this guy's garage."

XII.

The next day she had taken him to buy clothes, finding him surprisingly fussy about them. He chose a scholastic-looking zipper jacket and a checkered sport shirt with a button-down collar from a boutique in Westwood Village with origins in New England. All of the larger department stores, their dressing rooms seeded with pins, offered things like big pants with chains, an impiety that Peter wanted free of.

Afterward they ate lunch on campus. UCLA seemed quiet in summer but metropolitan compared to Signal Hill. A group of Asian students pedaled past sycamores in purposeful discussion. He longed to study again, make notes at a desk, leave the dead gulch of summer with its dirt on the straps of his sandals. The Metrolink commute come September he imagined as a Holy Land tour bus. Or he could carpool with the bass player from the club, a sophomore, who told him what professor to avoid for the class in Java Script.

This was exciting stuff. Back in Leviton's garage, working at a laptop computer on loan from the Back

Road, he was sleepless over the new life he'd glimpsed. He began mapping out a video game about it in the form of a maze. The university would be reachable by subterranean tunnels and secret warps from some carnal outlands of shipyards and bars. "Name it Big Game James," James urged him a few weeks later. "The big sellers are all character games."

"It's going to be called West L.A.," Peter insisted. He engraved the title into his spiral binder, girl-friend-style, a mistress of his heart.

He'd had a mistress of the heart once before. Her name was Daryn, and nobody even liked her until this guy Bryan did at school. She recognized something good in Peter and then she'd changed. He thought that she was bisexual, not that it changed how he felt. For about one night after running away he had wanted to be as unfeeling as she was. She used to know herself better than he had known himself, but not now. He saw her get fooled by popularity. Once, through Leviton's garage door, he heard her voice say, "I know, I look twelve," and he slipped back through the slat he'd pulled off the back of the garage and left through the space between two yards. Imagining she was deeply sad, he voiced a prayer in which Daryn was happy with or without him. He should never have admired her belief that they were dark and damaged. What mattered could not be destroyed.

He remembered how, when he was very small, he hid treasures in the dirt around his mother's rented house in Pacific Palisades. His father had told him to do something nice for his mother without ever taking credit for the deed — let her suppose she had an angel. It now seemed like a pretty great idea, although the stuff had gotten filthy. He was always making people gifts that came out wrong.

On the bedroll that smelled of Lucy's hair, her hashish, and her improvisations with James, Peter Gorski typed: *From Kent B. in Oregon. Dear Request Line. How about he's a male stripper, and she's having her bachelorette party? She only meant to get his autograph.*

The night was awfully still. He rocked forward onto his feet and emptied his pockets onto Leviton's workbench, loose change, plus a ticket he had bought on campus that read ASUCLA #222. It was for an upcoming Halloween dance, a group blind date. You'd wear the number on your lapel to meet your lucky partner — the two-hundred and twenty-second girl to buy a ticket, evidently. The unpunctual enchantress. And what was up with the three twos? It should have been a hand of poker. Then he could be lucky in cards, if not in love.

Soon the sun would rise. This was Peter's time, awake while others slept. He fantasized happily about his video game, letting details emerge like cities under clouds. Already he had decided that his protagonist would be nameless. Indeed, it would have no earthly form at first. But having survived the game's early trials, players would be granted an overhead view of themselves — a sort of astral third-personhood, as well as a perspective above danger. The trick of transcendence would be maintained by the player's own biofeedback (Peter loved this wrinkle, an evolutionary leap in gaming) — brain waves monitored by medical paraphernalia, everything attached by Velcro patches. That this could take years to pull together was a given. But the home stretch would all but paint itself: passage through the industrial prairie of the South Bay to a promised land based without apology on Westwood Village, a collegiate backdrop of scholarship and autumn splendor.

He was ecstatic when his early renderings of paradise came to life. He was dejected when the etchings would stare back as merely etchings. He wanted flower carts, vendors, that sense of patrician childhood he had seen with Lucy on the quads, as if the school were an academy for angels. But laced everywhere with shadows, temptations to doubt. Even the homeless of Westwood Village he wanted to flicker between angelic and, depending on the cloudcast, their old sorry selves. In a culminating Lady-or-Tiger riddle, a shoeless man calling himself the Mayor of Westwood—and resembling Big Game James, in the face—offered what might be the key to the city or a lunatic's treasure. By the time clock of the Back Road it became their friendly joke. "Big Game James," Peter Gorski sang through the dog days of August, affecting a workman's swagger, "the Mayor of Westwood."

XIII.

His mother was in full flower missing him. Each time before phoning, he felt beaten by the necessity of explaining himself, or politely evading her questions, a maneuver he had never quite accomplished that he could remember. If he tried to persuade her of his happiness, she would catch him in a logical mistake of some kind, and that would suggest he was not as free and clear and cloaked in the spirit as he'd hoped. She would stop arguing while his voice rose and he would hang up the phone, thus proving her point. He could forget about ever growing up then. She was cold earth, the single fear he had left.

He began the first call by dictating terms, reading these from notes like his own kidnapper. Certain subjects they must never discuss. Housing, for one. It would be best not to talk about housing. Nor would the length of his calls be negotiable, and she would hear from him again only in the event of an emergency, but he ticked off that edict in a voice that suggested he had already essentially waived it, and she prevailed upon him to shoot for once a week. Her position derived purely from the kingdom of nature: She needed the sound of her young. So he talked, although his voice fell flat and anxious when he offered it to his mother. "If I ever saw him," Jaimie told her hair colorist, "I would hit him and never be sorry. If I had just slapped him instead of arguing with him all his life, he'd be one of those strong silent types today."

"He seemed pretty silent to me already," Doralicia replied, spanking foil wraps with a flat comb.

"More like sweet. But if anyone raised their voice, he'd cry. He would look at you as if he were defenseless. When we took him for swimming lessons he cried, so we took him to the sink-or-swim school, and he sank, and he cried while he sank. I told him, I don't know who you are. I don't know how to reach you. He survives by curling up. He thinks that if he closes his eyes, everything bad will go away."

Brick red as she hadn't been in fifteen years, she worked half-days now, drinking vodka in a lawn chair on the driveway, grinding pebbles with her toes. The skyline of Long Beach could be seen below as a litter of parcels. The Boys and Girls Club of Signal Hill, to which Peter never belonged, had embraced her calamity, sending donations and a sculpture of a dolphin made from brambles and thorns. The clubmaster hung it on her wall and stayed for a drink. After the butts of their cigarettes had filled a pale green ashtray in the image of a kidney-shaped pool, he made a pass, and she gave in, as if to see exactly how empty she could feel; perhaps for that reason it hadn't felt completely empty nor unfamiliar. Whatever price the soul pays for loveless sex, she concluded she had paid it in her twenties; and what was loveless anyway? Who could fall low enough, who could find a darkness barren of love?

The clubmaster was also a volunteer fireman; now she had a host of civic friends. At a trucker bar at the foot of the hill she'd found them: the parents of Peter's old classmates and teammates from soccer, swingers, losers; all these years she'd lived among them and hadn't known.

Her block was a roadside attraction of weekend projects, boats on blocks and vivisectioned Harley-

Davidsons. On its side like a roped calf, the wedding canopy ranked as Jaimie Gorski's own exhibit, more Western-looking now because summer had bleached the grout to shades of salt. Seated with her eyes closed and sun searing her jawline, she saw herself a funny old curator, the kind who would charge admission and ladle water to tourists from a tub. Neighbors arrived daily with Igloo coolers, and she would sit beside them with one leg outstretched as if in a plaster cast. They drank into the night, and she sat so long that when she rose to get more drinks she limped. Chair, bikini, and earth, stiff as crusts.

Once, in a fugue of gallantry, Leviton called to check on Jaimie Gorski's condition and heard a block party's merriment on the line. Gorski sounded chatty and philosophical—Peter hadn't run away; he'd left for college three months early. He hadn't abandoned the whole world, she told Leviton—only her! She laughed, still deft with a masochistic dagger. Most surprising, Leviton's attentions seemed unneeded. He was glad of that, although hearing her garrulous and tipsy he felt estranged, curious what her summer was like, and how she had pieced herself together.

Dorothy, the Armenian library clerk, was due that night for a picnic, their fifth date. By an act of lunatic free will, he had wooed her. He had taken one heroic lunge at adaptation. You can push a lonely man just so far. You can bring only so many bare-scalped Jewish Electras into his lovesick embrace.

Had Dorothy not been an aunt three times over—a Gauguin figure, children on her barely formed lap—he could never have approached. They had bantered about children with his son in tow; he passed her a business card with a note suggesting dinner. Furtive and unsmiling, she thanked him for the card, then phoned him an hour later. "Are you *married?*" she asked deliberately, offering a dunce his opportunity to confess.

With Zachary she was visibly smitten. "So cute! Hello, Bopey." The name (was it short for Bo-peep?) voiced for her delight more than the child's, a feminine designation, a napkin positioned on a table.

The times he phoned she answered breathlessly, chaos in the background, feet pounding on stairs. The times she phoned, her *hello* sprang from her, as if she'd nearly lost him in the dark.

She caught him staring as she drove and said, "What?" Then he let adoration reign.

"What beach are we going to?" she asked him.

"Wherever you want. I'm happy just to be with you."

She looked skeptical. "You can't be this wonderful."

"Who couldn't, for you." He enjoyed this, how the grave words just came, his voice more than just his voice. Maybe this was all a man needed, to feel himself speak from someplace timeless.

The first date was a tapas bar in Long Beach. She thought he'd said *topless,* but consented anyway ("Do you take a lot of girls there?—"), afterward confessing her relief. The formality of her predicament made Leviton dizzy with lust. He was half-crazed from a season of protein drinks and calisthenics, muscled in tribute to his young flower. Biceped, the envy of men, though it felt ornamental on him, like a costume or a whisper of corduroy. She adjusted a vinyl miniskirt in the front of her parents' car until he crawled up and kissed her, lifting her face in his hands like the Hope diamond. She told him to stop, the neophyte role should be hers. For Leviton was good at romance by now, or ought to be. At least nothing could really surprise him.

Not that he didn't still love to love — and it was growth, a perk of maturity, to know that romance could be learned, mastered, hummed along with like a favorite old song. Though this alone washed away the sand-castle majesty of Leviton's youthful loves, when sexual promise seemed the contraband of a few local girls who possessed it, when a kiss on the mouth was as startlingly personal as hearing his own voice whisper from behind him. There was no such awe in midlife. He had loved, or thought so at the time; he was a father. Sex worked its hustle on men, left them fathers and moved on. It didn't care what happened next or in the end.

The sky was a milky magenta, the beach unlittered, but the combed sand gave off a recycled, industrial tang, and Leviton was struck by the absence of wind or waves. On a postcard it could have been a world-class resort, although which resort he didn't know. They shared anorectic bites of biscotti while he read from Thomas Hardy. She nestled back against him, perfect-figured, jeans like sand statuary — together they reminded him of the couple in a photo frame at WalMart. "I don't really under-stand poetry," she announced with her eyes closed, waiting to be kissed, his unpoetic WalMart gem.

She had told him how as a high-school senior she had won a scholastic achievement award from the Boys and Girls Club of Carson. That was for turn-ing her life around after shoplifting a pair of leop-ard-skin sandals in the seventh grade. The presenter of the award—a football coach from Stanford University distantly related to one of the clubmas-ters' wives—applauded her ambition to go to busi-ness school, adding that every child present could succeed by studying hard. Lightheaded on the dais, Dorothy asked if he could arrange to admit her to Stanford. She barely knew where Stanford was. The coach laughed nervously before leaving through a back door with a sports reporter. "I thought that if somebody like me ever met somebody like him, I was a fool if I didn't ask him to pull a string. Can you believe the embarrassment? I was so desperate to seem savvy. Now I just want to learn and make good money, and travel. Travel the world and not ask for any favors. Do you know what I mean?" She trailed a sandbag leg over Leviton's, eyes both catching and avoiding his, a sexy-shy performance. "I'm more practical than romantic, you know."

"Oh, you don't need to be romantic," he philoso-phized. "Only men are good at being fools."

"Women make mistakes too," Dorothy said. Her last boyfriend, for instance, she gave everything to, with saintly heartache. Her father warned her she'd be sorry. Her father loved her.

"But men make mistakes proudly."

"It's not about men or women. It's just me—I'm practical, not romantic." Playing with him. "I'm obsessed with you, though. Do you think I might be obsessed with you?"

"No one says that who is."

"I call you all the time."

"Oscar Wilde said, 'Great passion is the privilege of people who have nothing to do.' "

"Look who's unromantic now."

"No, I'm so taken with you I'm spilling my deepest fear. Against my better interests."

"Do the veins do that naturally?" She touched his bicep, feigning awe. "Have you been working out more?"

"You look very nice too."

"I like to be fit," she agreed, moving on to smooth the creases of his pants. Too high up the seam, snatching his breath. Once, she had asked him: "When guys dance slow, do they ever really, you know—in their pants? Or is that just an expression?"

"Now I definitely don't trust you. You're twenty-four years old! You know plenty."

"No I don't. I can't even bring myself to use the words."

"I don't believe you." Couldn't she be that sweet and his? Should he think so? Wasn't it the essence of romance to be a dreamer, to see what an objective view might miss? Or was that his whole problem?

"You could probably teach me to be some hot girl."

"You're making fun of me!"

"No," she said. Then kissed him slowly, like a healer.

Pouring from a thermos of coffee he talked about his day, about going to the Adamson House in Malibu with Zachary to look at the furnishings. She teased, "That sounds so boring. I will never be as boring as you. I like things that are nicer than you. Discos and guys who don't have beards."

She was unbuttoning his collar as he might have dreamed she would, as she might have seen someone do in a movie. They would be lovers soon enough, but this prelude itself approached nirvana. Only the relentless ease and comfort of the neighborhood struck him as odd, along with the eerie sound-stage calm. Desirable beach homes held the view across a boardwalk and there were tides, even despite the breakwater: water choppered to the sand with a rhythmic sound. But he felt banished somehow from real beaches, from spray filling the homes farther north in Malibu, from candlelit bedrooms with trunks draped in shawls. An onshore wind hurling the sky across the mountains. All his life he had sensed in the architectural chaos of Los Angeles that forces of nature were eternal while manmade temples were doomed: campfires and seacliff patios, chimneys of empty beer cans that were shrines to a party on the sand. Now the storms of the world seemed both here and gone elsewhere. The rains of winter had sent debris downriver that dried around them in fringes of litter.

To adapt himself to the time and his town he stroked her hairline—such a poignant region of the self, the forehead smooth, the strands' tough growth in spite of her, and so long as she would live. Dead matter that kept growing, that was strange. She would probably think it was unpristine.

When he got home late that night the phone was already ringing: her again, from her car, *Hello?!* — the astounding brightness of her voice. As if he'd found her popping up behind a door.

He entertained her questions like a screen star. *How long had he been divorced? Did he date a lot of women? Did he want to have more children? What was he doing now?* She herself was going upstairs. Nieces or nephews running by. She was unpacking something purchased just that day, an inflatable pool. She was hiding this phone call from her dad. "He says you want to fuck me," she whispered.

But he wanted only the best for her, he did. He would buy her a thousand inflatable pools just to watch her open them. He had the most unselfish aspirations to let love take its course, to protect it like a grape between his teeth — in the end he'd be the one to play the fool. She would outgrow him, Leviton assured her, she would come to resent his age; but he wasn't feeling so easy or detached reassuring her suddenly. He was slipping, daring to imagine them married, happy, blessed by angels. Dreaming that a man's foolishness could be his salvation. He was curling a dumbbell before the bathroom mirror, imagining her breasts, praying to St. Francis in the drumbeat of his lust to be an agent for somebody's good.

"I want a husband who wants to succeed," she sang, dreaming aloud. "I want to see the world."

XIV.

From her chair Jaimie Gorski let the sun pass. Toward San Pedro on the water in the form of a dumpling sat the geodesic hangar that once contained Howard Hughes's *Spruce Goose,* aviation's dodo. Long Beach below was a sandlot, the brown of low tide etched and wafered as if by her own fingernail. History Channel specials on the Holy Land often looked like that: panoramas of topsoil haunted by South American flutes. Forgotten battlegrounds.

Not that she could imagine Long Beach as a scene of biblical warfare. Road warfare, maybe, mercenary activity, bureaucrats and contractors driving as slowly as the possibility of arrival would allow, in a spirit of recreational malice. There would be lunch-hour brawls in the repair shops and strip clubs of Wilmington, halfcocked and giggling. Long Beach was a man's city, more like the blue-collar Madison of her youth than L.A., although as in many towns where men still did what they wanted, the women who stayed around had their pick of them. She had become somewhat fascinated by machismo. At the police station not long ago, paying for paperwork on Peter's disappearance, she saw a broad-backed man, a tattooed figure so quiet you could hear his breath in the hairs of his mustache, confront the Hispanic officer who'd arrested him for drunken driving. Eye to eye and in a menacing drawl, he announced that he had come to say thank you—"You turned my life around." Then strutted off as if followed by a train of attendants. Even the amends had been a piece of prison yard theater.

Yet she felt stripped lately of her judgment over anybody, this after a decade of feeling out of place in Signal Hill. Just the other day Richard Leviton had wandered into the trucker bar. That was a man out of place. He seemed in an agitated state, emerging from a taxi to phone some rabbi, and she tried to console him, an odd moment for she was already in costume for Halloween: a dancer's exotica of wedding veil, bikini, tiara, and scarves. She took him out back to shoot baskets — maybe the man needed friends and mindless fun. "There goes eternal youth," a customer winked over his beer, and she cracked, "I can pretend anything in a darkened room."

Leviton kept declining the basketball so she bunny-hopped about, flinging chest shots that banged off the backboard. Her cheeks were flushed with gaiety. "I don't know why, Richard. Not having any fun stopped being fun, or I'd still be doing it, I swear. I'm a hedonist. The saints are hedonists too, you know. They just have a more advanced idea of pleasure." She flipped the wedding veil and shrugged her shoulders. Leviton stared at the prickly stretch marks and the tan skin trickled with dry rivulets. "Every masochist is a hedonist at heart, or vice-versa. Oh, Richard. By the grace of God, if I could lighten you up, I would."

An ancient Dodge Colt arrived and Leviton got in. The vinyl front seat was insistent with the absence of Dorothy. Since becoming her lover he had felt her phantom come and felt it go. It was supposed to be that way for women, not men — the longing felt defenseless and feminine. She had worn thigh-high stockings and overwhelmed him: caressed him with her lips and hair, floated him up on the silent tension of her kisses. She had hovered over him ("Hop on pop," she teased), jumped around until he climaxed, and then she had rocked in slow earnest circles asking if she'd done anything wrong. In the morning she wanted guidance about UCLA. Effortless sex having apparently been covered in middle school. Leviton was at a loss — he hadn't been a student in more than twenty years; his last time visiting the university there'd been a rap concert at the foot of Bruin Walk, an MC declaiming "all my bitches" to a sea of love. Children really, aroused and corrupted by the liberal elite. "The peer-counselor from Mathematics never called me back," Dorothy fretted. Leviton swallowed hard before offering to hook her up with Daryn. He was a generous man, a man with hidden qualities, a man who knew eighteen-year-old girls. He could arrange for the three of them to get together. Where was the harm? In miserable self-consciousness he was dialing the phone.

It was Indian summer, hot even at 8 A.M. They dressed for the drive to Daryn's Westwood apartment with the smell of brushfires on the air. The domesticity of the place surprised Leviton at the door. It was a place where the details of shared living had been mastered. An older sister was wiping down the sunny kitchen and wrapping a baking dish of chicken. The living room had a view of the Los Angeles Mormon Temple, phallic, a stripe of oneness. On a rosewood shelf stood a panoramic class photo from Long Beach Wilson High; Leviton's eyes at once found Peter Gorski, stage left in a distant row of all boys. There were blue-ink inscriptions along the margins. (He nearly read aloud: "May you always stay a schoolgirl somewhat in disgrace.") On the coffee table, a framed photo had Daryn embraced by two girls on the hood of a car: cigarette bobbing at her lower lip, cheeks hollowing for a toke. Leviton the parent tried to pick out a decent driver among them.

Daryn led him away. "Don't look, I'm a monkey face. That is a face no one will soon love." She liked saying it. "My sister Renee is the beauty, and she won't let anybody touch her. As her math study group will attest. I tell her to let her hair down, just for the general morale." She gave a lowly laugh, but in her laughter Leviton could still see brightness, a monkey infant who has been her mother's darling.

Dorothy adjusted her skirt and did not glance at Leviton. She complimented the sister on an apron.

They had decided they could walk to campus, though it seemed twice as far on account of the heat, and Leviton kept looking behind as if they might turn back, the oasis of Daryn's building already invisible behind the rise of the Mormon Temple lawn and a railroad right-of-way. They marched through a construction site beneath humming power lines. They passed warnings tacked to trees about African beehives. Leviton's throat felt tacky — the air was so dry it whined. Why hadn't he asked for a drink of water? He could barely remember being indoors — the art books, Tolstoy and de Sade, the kitchen drawers that casted on ball bearings, a balcony of vines.

Soon they were on Westwood Boulevard, choosing the smoking patio in a health food restaurant, Leviton quaffing water and drawing smirks from the waiter as the girls shed their backpacks like the French. Daryn's was an army number from Israel. "No way! You've been there?" Dorothy was impressed.

Daryn looked straight at Leviton, lit a cigarette with the one she was finishing, and recited the story of her summer, as if to implicate him. "Well, my dad collapsed on a hiking trail and almost died," she said. "Because I couldn't remember CPR. Which he had taught me, twice. It was a normal vacation."

Her father had recovered, she said, but she had cried night after night like a guilty idiot. "Then at some point I decided I was done. I'm done trying to be good, or bad for that matter." She looked at Leviton as if only he would understand. "Here's an idea for you. We're stronger than God is, because our souls are as immortal as his, and we can reject him, too. He can't destroy what's been made. I was like: okay God, do what you will. Do your worst. I felt absolutely free. I spent the rest of the summer in Tel Aviv and I went totally lesbian, which taught me that I'm not a lesbian."

"Yuck!" Dorothy said without malice.

"They're so — I don't know — hung up on believing that they're freaks and that they've been disowned. Which is what they really wanted. They're selfish in a way. They have all these goddess statues in their apartments," she said, "and there's no majesty to them. We would hang around outside some bar pining about being two-timed by some girl, when we ought to have been home sleeping. There is nothing worse than being a woman who thinks she's in love."

Looking up from her menu just then Daryn seemed teary—adding a cryptic nobility to whatever suffering was behind what she had said—and Leviton nearly cried with her; in fact, he found it hard to look away. Was he ever that human or alive—God, was he falling for Daryn now too? Or was it the illusion of belonging that called out to him, the camaraderie of all lost children, of broken-heartedness embraced and childhood endured. He listened to the girls talking about study abroad, prerequisites, and nail-polish color all at once. He watched his twenty-four-year-old freshman (late for ambition but determined) through a haze of adoration and pride. But that was a distant, vicarious emotion, sealed off from the playing field of life. Could the subject of foreign study hold any firsthand wonder for him? Why did he feel that not only he but his whole culture had buried that Kennedy-era vision? Where, for God's sake, were the women his age?

Navigating the campus he was superfluous, a bear on a rope. Daryn was in charge now. Leviton devoted himself to people-watching. In keeping with the spirit of throwback, Jerry Brown, of all people, appeared—a crowd of reporters following him down the steps of a building in south campus—and by egotistical reflex Leviton drifted nearby, as if the newsmaker might remember with particular fondness a drunken wallflower of the press corps twenty years back. Lingering there, Leviton nearly lost sight of the girls jotting information from a math department bulletin case. He came up behind, meeting his reflection in the glass: not homely the way he'd feared, not the man who couldn't stop cutting his hair, but almost grotesquely dashing instead — thespian Leviton, smile sparkling, his hair full and blow-dried like a preacher's.

The girls had not missed him. They were reading things he could not make out through the ghosts of their faces in the glass. "They post your dance number outside Ackerman Ballroom on Halloween," Daryn told Dorothy. "You'll look on the men's wall for Number 222."

Dorothy cracked up repeating it through puckered lips, a mockingbird: *two, two, two.* Dorothy laughing was a beautiful thing to see.

XV.

"I know I'm losing her," Richard Leviton told the rabbi in a panic. "Even though I'm going to propose to her tomorrow."

They had parked the car and crossed Willow Street on foot, and the rabbi was trying to shimmy open any of the windows that faced his side yard. He had locked himself out again. "Isn't that odd?" the rabbi said. "How the stones throw off that turquoise reflection? Like Ipanima."

Leviton looked down at what he recognized to be scented cat litter. Even so he tested the pebbles with his heel to make sure he was not the one mistaken.

"You can see the box of doughnuts on the table. I wasn't lying."

"It's too hot for doughnuts," Leviton complained. He felt abused by the doughnut idea. He didn't know if the rabbi had paid attention to his problem. "I wonder if I'm kidding myself with this girl, but I do love her. And so I think, what's love for but to marry? To make something lasting. Does every match have to look right on paper? Not that she's all wrong. She's great with Zachary. She's an angel, if I think about it." Leviton began to smile through his agitation. "If I just think about it! Do you know what's good about me? I'm old enough to see that she's an angel in her imperfection. I can be good for her."

The rabbi shrugged. Leviton's complaint about suburbia had revived: That it was unromantic. That no one in Lakewood trusted you if you had ideas about living for a purpose. Or if you thought about the shallowness of modern life or even wanted to talk about anything like that. That whole boulevards of churches were set up to squash the religious impulse should it ever arise. He was better than them. He was a good man without a family, better than the ones who had the homes and marriages he ought to have had.

In his twenties Leviton had embraced his isolation, and he had found a narcotic kind of succor doing that. He had acted like romantic hope had died, and he'd been alive then. Jaimie Gorski had been as brown as a naturist and they were children, in a guest house, heirs to a city others had built, heirs to history. For a moment it seemed to him that freedom might be a location in Los Angeles.

So he'd thought to drive Dorothy and Daryn to Malibu where Jaimie Gorski used to live but could not find the house. The SUV broke down; Dorothy seemed to blame him. A tow truck moved them three blocks around a ravine—they were a hundred yards from San Vicente and didn't know it, just that close to the lush meridian. They could have rolled the car to the Unocal station. They could have gotten there by taking ten steps backward.

The ache of the freeway in a cab from Los Angeles to Long Beach in the heat is its own epic. In Brentwood and even Culver City one is held in the crush of an event, the Los Angeles phenomenon, a mass operation. The chaos is collective. Then the city recedes and the traffic in adjoining lanes begins to straggle. Maids in battered hatchbacks, gardeners with machinery roped in truckbeds. A clamor of tankers in the long long day.

"Whatever," Dorothy had said when he promised to call the next day.

"Marriage is a calling," the rabbi said after a moment. "Your other half calls to you before you know what it is that's calling out. 'In my bed at night I sought for my love, but I found my love not.' 'You have ravished my heart, my sister, my spouse.' You don't write the Song of Solomon twice in your life. Even if you feel it a thousand times. Because if you keep loving like that, you start wondering if your other half isn't wherever you find it. And then you resent God for being everywhere and nowhere. But if you're wanting her instead of Him, He disappears, doesn't he? It's about wanting to know your real calling."

"I do want to know! But I don't get called anywhere. I ask and I ask."

"As if you'd know that," the rabbi snapped. "You don't know how you're being used to help others. Not to call you a liar, but if you asked, you'd have received. You can't fool me on that one. Every moment that you're really asking for God's calling, you don't want anything else. You're already in heaven then. God's Kingdom spreads upon the earth. Just that fast. Bang-zoom. Want to know how to have no wants? Want nothing. But don't tell me you've done that. You don't even like anyone. You don't even respect your neighbors. Maybe you're starting to. Maybe God has a reason to lead you around by the penis. I don't know. God bless the women. Also wine and song, while we're at it. They're here, even though they're gone."

Leviton was confused. "Where is your wife?" he thought to ask.

The rabbi stared at him. "The only whole heart is a broken heart. The Rebbe Kotzher said that. She left five years ago. She left when I spoke in tongues."

Leviton groaned, loudly enough to be heard.

"And clapped my hands and barked like a dog. I was going to burn the house down. Burn it on the altar. So she left. You never saw me in the paper? I had a countdown on my web site—I was going to show it was only a house. She didn't like that. Women are of the earth, incidentally, in case you never noticed. Where's the wife in the terry-cloth robe, Leviton, when it's a hundred and fifteen degrees and you really need to get inside?"

"The house—didn't burn?" Leviton said stupidly.

The rabbi applauded. "I couldn't do it! And I still don't know—well, you don't want to know my problems. But I still don't know if it was God or the enemy who changed my mind. Because the house—it's a beautiful house, isn't it, and I thought, her spirit was in it. Love was in it. God is in it, is he not? With all its flaws. So I'm a captain, now, going down with his ship. Although the ship didn't technically go down. The window locks clearly work," he said bitterly.

Leviton was too weak to choose leaving or staying.

"Look, Leviton, this isn't your problem. It's hot. You wanted me to bless your marriage." He looked around as if for a place to kneel. Leviton hesitated above the cat litter.

"What on earth are these turquoise stones?" the rabbi asked sincerely.

"They're not gems," Leviton told him.

"Jews don't kneel anyway," the rabbi said, deciding the matter. "They don't speak in tongues either. You and I, we stand." He actually sounded Jewish now. "Lord, we thank you that our ways fail." He collected himself. "We pray for your blessing. But we don't mean it yet. Or we wouldn't have this *horseshit* going on." He banged on the windowpane.

"Oh help," Leviton said. It was the worst day of his life.

The rabbi stumbled, collapsed against the wall of the structure and just stayed there, ear to an invisible heart. Leviton was sure he smelled liquor.

"We'll say your prayer. We'll pray you have a happy hundred years with your beloved. Two hundred. Wedding presents. Silver trays, made to last and last." The rabbi stood still. "Maybe we should kneel after all."

Leviton searched himself angrily. "I thought you knew what you were doing." Next the rabbi would click his heels.

"No place looks like home. That's all right," the rabbi whispered. "Everything feels lost in the beginning."

Alan Rifkin's short stories have appeared in *L.A. Style* and *The Quarterly*. He has also written for the *Los Angeles Times Magazine, Details, Premiere, L.A. Weekly,* and *Buzz Magazine,* and was a finalist for the 2003 PEN-U.S.A. Award in Journalism. He lives with his wife and four children in Long Beach, California.